Second

L.A. Storm 2

RJ Scott

V.L. Locey

Love Lane Books

Copyright

Second (L.A. Storm, 2)

Copyright © 2024 RJ Scott, Copyright © 2024 V.L. Locey

Cover design by Meredith Russell, Edited by Sue Laybourn

Published by Love Lane Books Limited

ISBN - 9781785646270

All Rights Reserved

Blurb

Bryce has lost everything he loved. Michael is rebuilding a life built on lies. Is their love worth fighting for?

In the high-stakes world of professional hockey, Michael "Zeetoo" Zhang had the potential to shine brighter than his older brother, but he chose a treacherous path, and the scars of past failures and the constant shadow of his brother's success haunt him. He's had a run of bad luck, and is angry at the world, and his resentment intensifies when he's arrested, then sentenced to work supervised hours at an inner-city community garden. He's already lost hockey and his house; how can he afford to lose anything else?

Bryce Kincaid is chased by his own demons, and years after the mistakes he made, he's determined to never lose control again. He's built something stable and good from the wreckage of his life, and the last thing he needs is a pampered celebrity anywhere near his beloved community garden project. When Michael arrives, he's a broken man wrapped in a fiery package, but the gardens work their magic and reveal a vulnerability in Michael that Bryce can't resist. He's terrified to open his heart, and their growing relationship might be nipped in the bud.

To change his life, Michael must confront his past and fight for a future he's never believed he deserves. But when that past threatens to destroy everything Bryce has built, their love could be over before it's begun.

Dedication

To my family who accepts me and all my foibles and quirks.
Even the plastic banana in my holster.
VL Locey

Always for my family.
RJ Scott

L.A. STORM #2

SECOND

RJ SCOTT & V.L. LOCEY

Love Lane Books

Chapter 1

Michael

"CARD," I DEMANDED AND SCHOOLED MY FEATURES WHEN the king of diamonds turned up. I had a straight flush, and it was perfect—the kind of dream hand in poker that comes once in a lifetime. My heart raced as I peeked at my cards, barely containing my excitement. The odds were in my favor. It was a sure thing, a certainty, and blinded by the promise of winning, I did the unthinkable. I pushed all my chips to the center of the table. Everything. It was a bold move, a statement. I was all in. This was my moment, my chance to erase all my past mistakes, to come out on top, to prove to everyone, especially to my brother, that I was more than just a cautionary tale.

The room fell silent as the other players contemplated their next moves. One by one, they folded, until it was only me and one other—a newcomer with a poker face that gave nothing away.

The final card was dealt, and I held my breath, ready to claim my victory.

But fate, as I had learned the hard way, is often cruel. In a twist that seemed ripped from a movie script, the newcomer revealed his hand. It was the only one that could beat mine, a statistical improbability, a once-in-a-lifetime counter to my once-in-a-lifetime hand. A royal flush.

"Read 'em and weep, Freckles," my opponent cackled.

The realization slammed into me like a physical blow. I'd lost.

Lost everything. The room spun, and the sounds around me faded to a dull roar. I couldn't breathe, couldn't think. The chips, my lifeline, my ticket to paying my way out of debt, were now sliding across the table, away from me.

The weight of what I had done crashed down on me with brutal force. I'd gambled everything on a single hand, and everything was over. Paying off the debts, the promises of turning things around, the fleeting glimpse of a better future—all gone with the turn of a card—my brief taste of success was ash in my mouth. The debts were still there, looming larger than ever, and now, I had nothing left to pay them with. My car, my last asset, was as good as gone, promised to Looper for a fraction of its worth. I'd been so close to clawing my way out and keeping my baby, only to plunge deeper into the abyss.

"I'll be back," I said with confidence, but no one met my eyes.

I made my way through the smoky backroom to where Looper stood, overseeing his domain. The noise of the poker game faded behind me as I approached the man who held my fate in his hands. Looper, the enigmatic figure who ran these high-stakes games, was more than just a loan shark; he was a kingpin in this underworld, and he'd called me his friend for the longest time.

"Hey, Looper, buddy," I started, my voice brimming with the confidence of a man who'd had a win tonight before the losses. "I need more money."

He glanced up from his notebook, his expression unreadable, then flipped through worn pages with deliberate slowness, stopping at a page with my name etched at the top. His finger traced the figures next to it, a damning ledger of my debt. "You're in for sixty plus already, Michael," he said, his voice devoid of emotion, but his eyes were bright with excitement.

I swallowed hard; the euphoria of any win I might have had tonight weighed down by the cold reality of his words. "I know, I know," I rushed, "but you've seen me out there. I'm on a streak."

The air in the room grew heavy as Looper's eyes bored into me, a silent threat lurking in their depths. His calm demeanor belied the danger he represented, a façade of civility with his expensive suits and businessman vibes, masking the ruthlessness of a man who ruled whatever shadowy world he had going on here. It used to be I could play out in the open, or lay my bets in full view of anyone, but now... well, this was all I had. Shadows and deals.

"You're skating on thin ice, Michael," he said, then chuckled at his joke. "See what I did there, Mr. Hockey Hero?"

I stood my ground, trying for confidence, but inside, fear began to spike at what I was doing. Looper's reputation was well-known; he was not a man to be crossed. His words, though measured, carried an undercurrent of menace.

"Sure, funny. I get it." I paused. "Twenty K will cover me for now."

He raised an eyebrow. "I've been patient, but my patience has limits, and I'm cutting you off when I have debts against your name already."

As if on cue, one of his goons, the one with the accent— Kurgan, I recalled—a mountain of a man with a face like granite, took a deliberate step forward. The message was clear: this wasn't just a friendly warning. Looper didn't need to raise his voice or make explicit threats; his power was understood.

A bead of sweat trickled down my back. "I'm riding a wave of wins and I just need a little more time."

Looper studied me for a moment, his expression unreadable. "Time is luxury, and it's one you're running out of. Remember, I have eyes everywhere. I know about your wins, and I know about your losses. You can't hide from what you owe."

The reality of my situation was closing in, suffocating. Looper's presence, Kurgan looming silently behind him, were physical reminders of the threat hanging over my head.

"I'll get your money, Looper," I repeated, more to convince myself than him. "Just give me a bit more time. You know I'm good for it."

"Your worth is measured by your ability to settle your debts," Looper sneered. "And right now, Michael Zhang, you're worth nothing." His gaze was steady, and he closed the notebook with a soft *thud*, a gesture signaling the end of our conversation. "I run a business, not a charity, and time is something you don't have, Michael."

His words stung, but I was Michael *freaking* Zhang, and I was overdue some luck.

Looper tapped his lips. "But, say you throw me a bone on who's injured, or hey, what about you engineer the Storm losing to Boston next weekend…" Looper began.

"What?"

"A turnover here and there, a loss—that might pay me back some of what you owe?"

Shock nearly cut me off at the legs. "Fuck off. I'm not throwing freaking games." The thought of doing that, of letting down the team, of…

Would it hurt?

It would be one game.

Fuck. What am I doing? I'm not so desperate that I would do that.

Would I?

"The Storm is a team; it's not like I can throw a game just by my actions alone. You really think that I, alone, could make sure the Storm loses to a team like Boston?"

"But you'd be willing to throw a game if you could?"

"What? I didn't say that. No, I wouldn't help you."

"Then, that's your loss, Mr. Zhang."

I stood there; confident I could fix things. Looper's refusal to extend more credit was just a blip. The world I had been drawn into, this underworld of high stakes and higher risks, might be unforgiving, and didn't care about my potential, my earnings, or my name, but I was on a roll.

He *had* to see that.

"Fuck's sake, Looper—"

Kurgan placed a hand on my chest and the towering giant of a man was between me and my banker. I ducked and hip-checked him, but this wasn't some D-man I was skating away from, he was musclebound, had a hundred pounds on me, and was immobile.

"Leave," he grumbled.

I poked the bear, literally, shoving at solid muscle. "You need to fuck off, so I can talk to your boss."

Kurgan grabbed my hand, twisted it, and shoved me backward until I met the wall. Then, in a flurry of motion, he had me outside the side door, shoving me so hard I stumbled back and hit the scaffolding currently gracing both this building and the restaurant beside it.

I beat on that closed door—felt a bone crack in my hand I smacked it so hard—but I didn't care, and no one came out to me.

"Fuck you!" I shouted up at the building, a wave of righteous indignation washing over me. I crossed to my Mercedes, which was all flash and style, and about the only thing I still had to my name, even if the repayments were killing me. I kicked the tire. "Fuck you!" I repeated, drawing a few glances from pedestrians heading into the family restaurant.

Their expressions pinched, they had no idea how badly I'd been screwed over, or why I was kicking my car and railing at the world. I confronted them, bristling, waiting for them to say something, alcohol blurring the edge of good decision-making. I climbed into my car, the cool air doing little to dull the alcohol buzz, but knowing I shouldn't drive. I fumbled for my phone—looking for someone to collect me.

Someone who even cared about me enough to get here.

Not my brother. No, Charles *Golden Boy* Zhang would judge me, tell me I was messing up, demand I stop. Defiant anger simmered within me. I wasn't going to lie down and accept Looper's judgment, or my brother's self-righteous condemnation bordering on pity. People needed to remember my successes on the ice, that I shone bright, and the world freaking owed me.

I would win again, prove them all wrong.

Fuck that noise. Maybe someone on the team. Who? I couldn't think—my head hurt. Maybe Cam would throw me some cash, or Prez—both of them had contracts bigger than mine, and we were teammates—brothers-in-hockey—so they'd help? A renewed sense of determination flooded me at thinking of a way out. I pushed the button to get my phone working, only it was dead, because of course it was, and I turned on the car, then cursed and fought to get the charging lead working.

Startled, I turned towards a flash to my left. There, not more than a few feet away, was a figure with their phone out, snapping photos through my car window. The sudden intrusion felt like a violation, and my temper spiked. The light was blinding, disorienting, adding to the surreal sense that even my private temper wasn't safe from prying eyes.

I lowered the window a little. "Hey!" I barked, my voice laced with frustration and a hint of desperation. "Get lost!" But the guy, no more than a kid, undeterred by my outburst, continued to snap away, or was he filming now?

In a haze of frustration and the need for a swift escape, I threw the car into reverse and the engine roared to life. My hand was heavy on the stick, driven by the urgent desire to get away from prying eyes and flashing cameras.

The car lurched backward with more force than I'd intended, and before I could fully grasp what was happening, there was a sickening crash. The rear of my beautiful car collided with the scaffolding. People screamed, there was shouting, but for a moment, time seemed to stand still. The light from the camera was replaced by the flashing on the car's dashboard, warning signals blaring in the sudden silence following the collision.

I was okay.

I hadn't hurt myself.

Then, the scaffolding shifted, a cacophony of bending, breaking, and crashing.

And everything went dark.

I SLOUCHED IN THE STIFF LEATHER CHAIR AS, ACROSS from me, my lawyer Mr. Jenkins, adjusted his glasses, ready to dive into the grim reality of my situation. Beside me, Charles sat with his hands in his lap, silent, judging, and with a permanent expression of concern more patronizing than comforting.

"This is bullshit," I snapped because, yes, it was fucking bullshit. "It's not as if I hurt anyone apart from myself—no people were injured in the filming of me fucking up." I chuckled to myself, and Charles muttered under his breath. I didn't catch all the words, but I got the gist of his disapproval.

"Let's be clear about what's at stake, Michael," Mr. Jenkins began, his voice stern, yet not devoid of empathy. "Your sentence following the incident with your car is community service. This is non-negotiable."

"We need to appeal."

Is it hot in here?

"You did the crime, and we're not appealing," Charles snapped.

"Fuck you, Charles."

"You want to go back out there and appeal against something you know was wrong? How's that going to work?"

I glanced at Charles, biting back a retort. His presence was a silent reprimand, his involvement in my affairs a reminder of how far I'd fallen. Only by his grace was I even sitting in this office and not being driven to some prison in the ass end of nowhere. He'd paid for the best lawyer; he'd vouched for me; he'd basically thrown himself at the mercy of the media to defend me.

I guess it'd look bad for him if a Zhang brother was behind bars.

That was Charles—always watching out for number one. Asshole.

"And that's not all," Mr. Jenkins continued, speaking right over my incredulous sigh.

"Of course, it isn't." I slumped even further in my

seat. Three months, and the fall from grace had been spectacular. I was on long-term injured reserve, but it was only a matter of time before the Storm got rid of me, going the same way as my agent, who'd dropped me like a hot potato.

"Your driver's license is suspended for a year, but you don't automatically get that back. You'll have to go through assessment for sobriety."

"I'm not a fucking alcoholic; it was one drink!" Or two, or whatever. "I'm a professional athlete. I take care of myself."

Charles huffed and, I swear, he was one more huff away from me decking him.

"As for your living situation," Mr. Jenkins ignored my sobriety comment, "your sentence mandates living at the address on court records."

"My house," Charles said. He was trying for supportive, but I knew, that under that, he was probably feeling smug and self-righteous. "I'm his brother."

"I'm in the pool house." A cramped space, one-bedroom, a kitchen-diner, and shitty WiFi, a far cry from my sprawling house that had long since been sold off to repay the mortgages I'd taken out on it. "Shitty, small, and no AC."

"It's a roof over your head, and it's free," Charles said cautiously.

"Whatever, Saint Charles."

Charles gaped at me. "You're an asshole, Mikey."

"Fuck you," I snapped back.

Mr. Jenkins shuffled papers and cleared his throat, probably confused by the fact that fan favorite, captain of the LA Storm, Charles Zhang was an asshole, and I was having to stand up for myself. "With respect to the community engagement, there are limited choices for your placement, which you will begin in ten days. Details will follow shortly, but we do have a place for you."

"As I said, whatever."

"Michael, I know this is hard, but it's an opportunity to reset your life on a better path," Charles interjected, his voice laced with a sincerity that only fueled my irritation.

I turned away, his words feeling like salt in a wound. His life was perfect—Clare, his loving wife, two beautiful daughters, a successful career playing the game he loved. And here I was, losing everything because no one had ever given me the same chances my brother had enjoyed. I'd always been second best, not quite the player he was, not as old, not first in the line for the good stuff. There again, I was *just* the adopted kid; he was the one with the parents who'd actually created him.

"As I was saying, the place the team has in mind is a community garden project—a chance to contribute positively, as per your sentence," Mr. Jenkins said, snapping me back to reality.

I scoffed internally. From promising athlete to

gardener—not exactly the life story I had in mind. Still, once I was back, I'd show everyone how much Michael Zhang could win at life, and all I needed was the stake for the game.

"And of course, in September, in addition to the hours agreed for your sentence, you are mandated to spend five hours per week with The Honor Guards, the veterans' hockey team out in Encino. This was agreed with NHL Player Support as a way to—"

"Yeah, yeah, make it look good for them."

"That will be good for you too," Charles commented. "To work with vets and see what a real hero looks like."

I rounded on my brother, who reared back. "The fuck?"

He held his hands up in mock surrender. "All I meant was, hockey players aren't heroes; we're nothing special."

"Speak for yourself, asshole," I muttered. *And fuck you, big brother.* Living on his dime, freaking gardening, then, adding in hockey wannabes, and my punishment was complete.

"And remember, any failure to comply with these conditions will land you back in court," Mr. Jenkins concluded.

"Yeah, yeah, let's get this shit done."

Chapter 2

Bryce

"… AND THEN, UNCLE TONY AND I WENT HIKING. JUST us men. Mom stayed at the cabin to work on her new cookbook with venison meat. Dad, did you know that venison meat is from a deer?"

I smiled at my son via our weekly video chat, wishing upon wishes he could stop quoting *Uncle* Tony. Tony, or as he liked to spread it around, Wildlife Conservation Officer Anthony Langella, was my ex-wife's boyfriend. He was not Leo's uncle, and more importantly, he was not his father. *I* was his father. I might be a lame one, but I *was* his father. And if Tony, in his spiffy uniform and his trips to Red Rock Canyon Park where he worked and cared for wild animals and camped and sang songs around carefully tended campfires and spent every day with—

Slow that roll, Bryce. Leo loves you. Tony is good for him and Courtney. Jealousy is a petty, acidic emotion. She

16

deserves someone stable in her life. Your son will always be your son no matter how many desert big horn sheep or wily coyotes Tony shows him. You're just as cool. LA is just as awesome as a national park. If you squint really hard.

"Yeah, I did know that, bud. Did you like the venison stew Mom made?"

"I liked it okay. The carrots were gross, but Tony says that if I want to be a forest ranger like him someday, then I had to eat vegetables. Dad, when do I come to the garden again?"

"Well, that's kind of why I called, other than to talk to you. Is your mom around? We need to talk about you coming out for your Easter break."

"Yay! Dad, when I come out, can I feed the tent people carrots?"

Oh, my stars. He made it sound like we were running a petting zoo.

"Sure, we can pass out extra produce to the unsheltered people who visit," I corrected gently.

"Cool. I like them. That one lady, Ruth, gives me marbles. *Mom!*" he bellowed, making me wince. "Dad is on the computer for you!" His attention came back to me. "Will you fly out to meet me, or can I fly out alone?"

"Someone will fly with you. Mom and I will discuss all of that."

"I'm big enough to fly alone. Melissa Meyers flies to Arizona to see her grandma all the time alone, and she's a girl."

"Leo, what did we discuss about using that phrase?"

His sigh was so heavy it blew some of the dirty blond hair from his soft blue eyes, which he'd gotten from his mother. He wasn't much like me, apart from having my chin—hadn't inherited my warm skin tone, or black hair, not even my dark brown eyes—there wasn't a trace of my heritage in him at all.

"That girls are just as culpable—"

"Capable."

"Right, capable as boys of doing everything in the world. Here's Mom." He blew me a kiss, then raced off, probably to go play with Melissa, his friend, next-door neighbor, and instigator of flying alone when one was only seven.

Courtney appeared on the screen, her soft blonde hair pulled into a ponytail, her nose smeared with tomato sauce, and her bright white apron covered with ruby red speckles. She was adorable. As always. Even though we'd parted on less than amicable terms, I could admit she was a lovely woman, a terrific mother, and a wonderful cook. Her taste in men left a bit to be desired. I mean, she did pick me…

"Hey, Bryce," she said as she sat down, then rolled her chair back. "I'm glad you called. Is there any way that we can switch Leo's visit with you over Easter to something later in the year? Maybe a longer summer visit?"

My first instinct was to react. Something I'd

learned, over time and many months spent in meetings at NA, to tamp down.

"Courtney, I haven't seen him since Christmas," I reminded her. Not only that, but her brother, Jack, had visited them for two weeks' vacation just a month back, and boy hadn't I heard all about how wonderful Uncle freaking Jack was, with him being a cop, and having a badge, and putting bad guys in jail.

Good for Jack.

"I know, and I wouldn't ask, but Tony has this great idea to take us all to a seminar in Wyoming where we could finally get to visit Yellowstone, and Jack has already helped us out." I exhaled, hoping breath would purge the resentment of Tony the Park Ranger taking my time with my son, and Jack-the-awesome-uncle being all hero-like. "You look mad."

"I'm not mad. I *am* incredibly disappointed. I assume that Tony has mentioned this possible trip to Yellowstone to Leo?"

Her slim brows tangled. Whoops. That was not the right direction to take. Seems I'd know what pissed my ex off by now, she'd spent most of our married years angry at me.

Oh, you know perfectly well what buttons to push, don't be coy.

Yeah, I did, and it was petty.

"No, Bryce, he did not because he didn't want to build up expectations in case you threw yourself over this."

19

"I'm not sure that expressing my unhappiness over not seeing my son can be called throwing myself."

"Bryce." She closed her eyes, then opened them slowly, the anger lessening to be replaced with sad resignation. "I know you dislike Tony." I said nothing. She huffed. "Fine, let's not discuss Tony. Let's discuss if this is something that you're going to get upset about. If you want to be a dick about this then fine, we'll blow this incredible opportunity to show your son one of this country's most incredible natural places so he can sit in the middle of Los Angeles with you and those bees you're so fond of while people are carjacked on the corner."

"Bees are pollinators," I replied dully. She hit me with a flat look. "No, no, of course not, I'm not going to deny my son that chance. But I want him to spend the entire summer here with me." That wiped the smile growing on her face clean away.

"Bryce, that's a bit unreasonable. Besides, he's signed up for little Rangers camp in July, then Tony and I are taking him to Tony's parents in Florida in August to do Disney. Surely, you don't want me to cancel all of those plans so that he can feed the homeless limp carrots."

"They're homeless people, and my carrots are far from limp," I snapped back, then folded in on myself. "Fine, but I do want extra time. Two more weeks."

"Okay, sure, that's fair. Thanks for not making this a thing, Bryce."

"Of course." I gave her a feeble smile.

"Oh, and great news!"

"What?"

"Jack transferred your way, working out of the city. Not sure where, but close."

Oh great. Not. He would never forgive me for what I'd done to his sister and nephew; how in his eyes, I was a loser who'd destroyed any happiness. He had a point, but still, we were never going to be friends.

"I have to go, there's a pot," I mumbled, then said goodbye before ending the call. Sitting in my small apartment a block from my beloved garden, I let myself have a moment of pure ire. Then, because anger did a soul no good, I took a cleansing breath, changed into some loose pants and a bright blue tee with dancing tomatoes on the front, and shoved my feet into some old sneakers. I needed to de-stress, and the best place for that was the garden.

Stepping out of my cramped place, I locked up, then headed down the stairs and past the landlady's apartment. Hearing Mrs. Cho speaking to her cat, I decided to sit on the stoop and wait for her. City kids pedaled by on bikes, the flurry of different dialects from open windows floating by. Nary one carjacking occurred while I waited for my landlady to appear.

"Morning, Bryce," Mrs. Cho called as she backed out of her door, shooing her cat Lefty back before slamming the door closed. Lefty was an indoor cat now, since the day two years ago when he'd returned from prowling the streets beaten to bits by another cat. He'd ended up losing his left eye, which was why he was now called Lefty. Before me, he had been some random alley cat with no name. Now he was a fat yellow tabby with no balls and one less eye but possessing a full belly and a lap to curl up on.

"Morning, Mrs. Cho," I replied, smiling down on the diminutive woman with silver hair and a tiny nose holding up her always smudged glasses. Tiny she may be, but she was a force to be reckoned with when needs be, and she was also one of the kindest, most giving people I'd ever met. Not everyone would have rented their upstairs apartment to an ex-addict who had zero references, zero job opportunities, and zero chances. "Did Lefty eat the salmon that Miles brought to the garden?"

"No, that stupid cat. He eats plastic bags, but not canned salmon." She headed out, little feet in crisp white sneakers, her goal the community garden and our weekly sunrise tai chi class.

"Sounds like a cat," I chuckled after increasing my pace to catch up. "Although, to be fair, I have no clue where Milo found that can of salmon or how old it was."

"Seems an old alley cat wouldn't be so picky," she replied, turning left at the fruit market. We waved at Bohdan, the owner, stopping only for a moment so Mrs. Cho could buy a Red Bull. Bohdan was a big man from Ukraine who had settled here many years ago with his wife. She had passed ten years ago this spring, and ever since, Bohdan had been trying to woo Mrs. Cho, who had also been widowed for a decade.

I chuckled at the two pretending they didn't notice the other. I'd been alone ever since my divorce, and if someone—male or female—stared at me the way Bohdan looked at Mrs. Cho, I'd be in his or her arms in a flash. Of course, that kind of impulsive behavior was a large reason I'd ended up divorced and alone, so yeah…

The walk to the gardens was a short one as we lived nearby. Mrs. Cho spotted him first, as I was digging my keys out of the pockets of my linen pants.

"Who is that stud?" she asked, skidding to a halt in front of me. I nearly rear-ended her, avoiding a crash with a neat sidestep that bounced me off the tall fencing around the San Pedro Street Community Garden. My gaze found the man in question. He was parked in front of the garden gates, his backside resting on the bumper of a brand-new Subaru Forester, his long legs crossed at the ankles. He gave the impression that he was bored with the world, arms folded over a snug gray tee that showed off his thick biceps. Damn, he was gorgeous—I'd always had a thing for redheads. "He looks like my Ha Joon when he was young."

Since I'd never met Mr. Cho at any age, all I could do was nod. Lucky Mrs. Cho if her hubby was that handsome. She called over to the stranger in Korean. He ignored her and stared back at the small group of people waiting outside the garden, most in comfy clothes, a sneer on his face. We had ten seniors who followed the class led by Mrs. Cho and me, and they were all here, along with a few homeless people waiting for some goodies. The stranger had no need to be sneering at anyone.

"Ah, pity he's rude; still, he's a looker. You should hit him up," she whispered. I didn't want to defend the sneer, but he probably didn't speak Korean. Mrs. Cho poked me in the side so hard I swore she cracked a rib. "You like the boys, and he's a hot-cha-cha."

I felt a blush rise up my neck, and wished I hadn't decided a week back to shave my beard, which would have hidden it. I was scruffy, according to Mrs. Cho, and so, off it had come. "I like boys *and* girls," I reminded her, then gave the people outside my garden gate a warm welcome. "Sorry we're running a little late. I was visiting with my son online, and he likes to gab." I flung the gate open wide.

All the seniors cooed about Leo as they entered. The unsheltered waited outside, as they always did. They were more than welcome to come in, but they seemed happier staying on the sidewalk with the possessions they carried. Most packed up their tents and carted them along with them, if they had tents, since the city sanitation department would sweep through and dispose of their belongings. It was a terrible practice, I felt, but I had little control over what the city did to counter the situation, even if I did show up at city hall to protest such things. Sadly, no one seemed to have any real solutions to the problem of the homeless in this or any major city. So, we did what we could for those we could. I'd done my share of sleeping on the street before I'd gotten clean, and had stumbled into Mrs. Cho, who seemed to have a soft spot for unwanted strays who slept on her stoop.

"Hey," Mr. Handsome called as he loped into the garden, his pale eyes sweeping the large area as if he expected a monster to leap out at him from the Chavez family's corn plants, which were doing quite well, even with the lack of rain of late. "I'm looking for the garden manager, some Bryce guy?"

"That would be me," I answered, motioning for Mrs. Cho to get the class going while I opened the small office building. "Are you the electrician the main office sent out to check on the sprinklers in the greenhouses?"

"What? No, I'm not the electrician. I'm Michael Zhang."

I flipped on the light switch inside the stuffy brick building. The overhead fans whirred to life, pushing warm air down over us. The way he'd said it implied I should know who he was.

"I'm sorry I don't…" *Oh, wait. Zhang.*

I stared hard at the man, which wasn't a hardship because, damn, he was fine. Pale and freckled, his red hair was styled short and close, and his pale eyes were winter-gray on closer inspection. I'd been a happy bisexual for most of my adult life, and while my experiences with men had been few, they'd been freaking incredible. Then, I'd kind of gotten married, fell off a stage in Seattle and totaled my knee, got hooked on pain killers, weaned myself off the pills, and that led to… well, shit, that didn't need to be hung on the mental lines to air out right now.

"Oh right, the hockey player." The one I'd signed off on allowing him to serve his time here a few weeks ago. My memory was poor on a good day and atrocious on a bad. I liked to blame old age and a misspent youth.

"Yeah, *the* hockey player." I paused to digest the snark in his tone. "I have to show up here for three hundred hours, so can we just get started. The sooner I get this asinine punishment done and over with, the sooner I can return to trying to get back on the team roster and leave this shitty dirt patch behind."

"Wow, okay, so before we even get started here, let me explain a few things. I get that you're coming here against your will, but if you call my garden a shitty dirt patch again, I will toss your ass to the curb faster than you can say Roma tomatoes." He stared down at me with another sneer, as if he doubted I could toss him anywhere, and while I *was* in shape, I suspected he was right. "Also, if you continue to fling your attitude around at me or the others who volunteer here, I *will* make a note of it on your paperwork." All the sass left his face. "Oh yes, I do report back to the court via a weekly call or email, so why don't you chuck that arrogance into the compost bins. Are we clear, Mr. Hockey Star?" He nodded. "Good. Now let me find you a T-shirt that fits, you can answer some questions, and then can get to work. We're adding fertilizer to the pumpkin patches today."

The look I got from him was priceless. Nothing brought a man down from his self-righteousness like working cow shit into the earth.

Chapter 3

Michael

Bryce had a clipboard in his hand and a smile that wouldn't quit—until it was replaced with that spark of temper. He was attractive, with a rugged charm that irritated me for reasons I couldn't quite understand. His warm welcome and easy demeanor felt like a stark reminder of the chaos of my own life, but his stare was judgmental, his frown so deep I thought it might scar his face. His skin was tanned, his dark hair shining, gorgeous eyes full of life, and I wondered if he might have some Pacific Islander blood judging by his features. I was caught by the sight of earrings in one ear as his dark-eyed gaze focused on me, checking me out from head to toe.

Checking me out? Or *checking me out?*

"This way," he said, then pivoted and headed off, expecting me to follow.

For a brief moment, I considered staying where I

was, but what would that achieve toward me working off my time?

Bryce led me through the garden, and for some godforsaken reason, he slowed so I was walking next to him, and then, worse, he began to explain what was here with a passion that seemed foreign to me. His enthusiasm for something as mundane as gardening grated on me, and resentment I even had to listen to this grew with each step. In fact, the more Bryce spoke, the less I heard, as my mind fixated on the life I should be living. The Storm was playing the Raptors tomorrow—always the best game with our closest division opponents. We'd met them three times already this season, won once, and tomorrow was supposed to be payback.

Only, I wouldn't be playing.

Sucks to be the Storm when they lose because I'm not there. A loss would show everyone just how ineffective Charles was at being captain when they failed without me. Not that they'd lost much over the past three months of me not playing, but they'd realize what they were throwing away if they converted my long-term injured reserve status to shoving me out altogether.

As Bryce continued his overenthusiastic tour through the garden, which was—apparently—the best community garden in the history of whatever the hell whenever, I found my attention wandering. The drone of his voice became background noise. His words on composting techniques and the importance of crop rotation fell on deaf ears. I nodded along, not even trying to feign interest, while inside, resentment simmered.

Bryce, with hands animated as if painting a picture, had moved on to the people who used the space, and for some inexplicable reason, he included a treatise on the garden's bartering system. "We trade what we grow here for other goods," he said with pride. "It's not just about the harvest; it's about building a community, you know?" I nodded, as he talked about the exchange of tomatoes for fresh eggs, or herbs for honey. That was archaic—hell, who couldn't afford a few freaking tomatoes?

Bryce ushered me back into the office that was nowhere as tidy as the order outside, and I took a good look around. This room—more like a shed really—was cluttered and messy—shelves filled with empty plant pots, boxes piled in the corner, and the air stunk with the earthy smell of greenery, and the damp in here made me gag. God, I missed the ice.

I took a seat, the chair creaking under my weight, and watched him clear space on his desk, then rummage into a drawer, coming back up with a clipboard, then running his fingers through his short dark hair.

"First thing's good news," Bryce started, his tone casual, but professional. "I printed off your background check report and it was clear."

"Apart from almost killing an entire restaurant of families," I said, pushing him to react.

He frowned. "DUI is what I have here."

"I could have killed someone." I sat forward in my chair, daring him to ask me more.

"But you didn't," he said, all calm and matter-of-fact.

I hated that he could sit there and know all about me when I knew nothing about him. I bet he hadn't known a day of trouble in his entire life, same as my sainted brother; probably had family who told him he was a great guy and did this work because he could fall back on Daddy's trust fund.

Or Mommy's—I was an equal opportunity trust fund accuser.

"Back to this, then," he said. "We have a responsibility to the community, especially since many of our attendees are vulnerable."

"'Vulnerable', huh?" I mumbled because I'd lost the chance of a confrontation with this do-gooder who'd ignored me trying to get him to react.

Bryce flipped through his clipboard, ticking off items with a pen. "All right, Michael. Mike? Mikey?"

"Michael is fine."

"Okay, a few routine questions for our records," he began. "We don't allow smoking on the property, nor drugs. As to drinking, you will be subjected to random checks, and it's a one-strike and you're out policy."

"I can take or leave drink," I said, and he raised an

eyebrow. "The fucking DUI was just another shitty piece of bad luck in my already shitty life," I added, and he returned my gaze with a steady focus. I felt as if he was waiting for more. "What about poker?" I asked.

He frowned. "No regular poker games here, I'm afraid."

"Shame, because I'm down the two years left on my contract, and I could do with getting the eight mill back."

He didn't flinch at me throwing around my contract amounts—four mill a year—which I'd now lost, but whatever, I used to be someone, until it had been taken from me.

"Well…" he drawled, and his voice pulled me back to the conversation. "We do have some pretty intense composting competitions," he deadpanned.

For a moment, I felt a bubble of a laugh inside me at his joke. I had words on the tip of my tongue that I almost said. "I'll keep my poker face ready for that, then." I didn't say a single thing.

Instead, I sneered.

He shook his head and returned to the form. "There are protocols in place for your safety, which I will be taking you through a step at a time. Most importantly, you will be working outside, in the sun, and you *will* cover up and use the highest factor cream available." He glanced up at me, and I knew what he saw—red hair, freckles, pale skin, easy to burn.

"I'm not stupid, I cover up," I snapped. "You think I keep this good-looking by accident?"

He ignored that. "Each full hour you work will be marked from these pages in the folder," Bryce explained, tapping a printed sheet. "I'll need to sign off on each one and file a detailed report to your probation officer of what you achieved."

I raised an eyebrow. "Got it. So, you're going to jot down every time I plant a flower or shovel manure?"

He ignored me.

Bryce dragged a box from the corner of the office, filled to the brim with long-sleeved T-shirts bearing the garden's whimsical logo—an eggplant and a cluster of fruit. "Here," he said, "find one that fits."

I pulled out a shirt, eyeing the logo. "Nice eggplant," I quipped, the sarcasm in my voice unmistakable.

"We get what we're given," Bryce replied with a shrug, unfazed. "Budget doesn't stretch to fashion statements."

I stripped off my designer tee—one of the few things that was still mine—letting it fall to the chair, aware of Bryce's presence in the small room. I didn't have issues getting undressed in front of someone, hell, years in locker rooms taught me that no one was checking me out however hard I flexed and posed.

Although I did peek at Bryce to see if he was indeed looking as I revealed skin. I flexed my muscles because I wasn't above a bit of showmanship, even if it was for the indifferent eyes of a man who seemed more interested in compost than a six-pack. Still, as I pulled the snug garden shirt over my head, I thought for a moment I saw a glint of something in Bryce's eyes, but all too quickly he returned to professionalism and indifference. The shirt hugged my pecs a bit too snugly for my taste, and only just skimmed my belt. I yanked it down, then took it off and rummaged around in the box for a larger size, finally happy to find one that didn't ride up when I touched my toes.

"We have yoga," Bryce blurted, then shuffled the papers on his desk back into the folder with my name on the outside.

"Huh?"

"Morning yoga, for when you get here at six-thirty a.m."

"I'm guessing morning yoga doesn't count toward my hours?"

"No."

"Then, I won't be here for six-thirty a.m.," I argued.

He tapped the file. "Mandated hours, six a.m. until four p.m. Your choice on yoga but sitting it out is you just wasting time."

"I'll dig shit while you do yoga."

"Not unsupervised you won't."

"Then, I'll get here for seven."

"You'll be here at six or that's an issue I'll be taking up with your probation officer." Impasse, but I'd get my lawyer onto it. "You'll take two fifteen-minute breaks morning and afternoon, and there is one hour for lunch."

No, I won't. I ignored all the breaks because I wouldn't be taking them. I was getting these hours knocked down as fast as I could. The only concern I had was calculating how in God's name I was going to get here at six, what with not being able to drive. Not that I even had a car, and a twinge of grief at the death of my Mercedes gripped me. I'd loved that car, but when the firefighters had finished cutting her up to get her out of the scaffolding nest, she was nothing but scrap, and the insurance money went toward my debt on the house.

Charles would have to drop me off—get his ass out of his cozy bed in his huge house and drive me here. I chuckled at the thought, and Bryce frowned at me. My bad.

"Okay, let's start," Bryce said after a pause, his voice pulling me back from my moment of grief for the past me who'd messed up. "Pumpkin patch is this way." He left the office expecting me to follow without hesitation. I trailed behind him and stared at his ass as he strode down pathways to a large plot of land about as far from the office as possible. Deposited in one corner of the expanse of mud was the biggest pile of shit I'd ever seen, the stench a harsh reminder I was not at an ice rink anymore.

Fuck my life.

As Bryce and I dug into the garden work, I couldn't

help but notice he was strong—his shirt tightened over his bunching muscles with each movement, and I caught glimpses of skin as he leaned forward. It was a straightforward recognition—the guy was in shape, and it showed—it was just a shame about the preaching about the environment that came with the sexy ass and muscles.

As the day progressed, my irritation grew. Bryce's instructions, his casual chats with other volunteers he introduced me to—it all grated on me. Every time he smiled or laughed with them; I felt a surge of annoyance.

I could do the hours they gave me.

And when I left, I'd bury Bryce and his infrequent-but-annoying lectures about sustainability in the pumpkin patch with all this freaking manure, so deep they'd never find his body.

Exhausted, I took a moment to check my watch, expecting five hours to have passed.

One.

One solitary hour.

Fuck. Freaking hundreds of hours to go.

Chapter 4

Bryce

Okay, yes, I know, snickering to yourself as you spied on the newest volunteer trying to figure out how a hoe worked was petty. Color me childish then. Courtney would agree. She always said I acted worse than Leo at times.

Still, I lingered in the shade by the hives—a place where few tended to hang out because… bees—and watched Michael *the* hockey player attack a plot that had been returned to us as the renters had moved. He wasn't working the packed-down soil so much as he was trying to chop it into bits. After ten minutes being a sniggering ass, I moseyed on over to Michael assaulting plot number fifteen.

"Do you have something against this section of soil?" I asked as he dug down into the dirt with enough force to fell a mighty oak. He was soaked in sweat, which was not a bad look at all for the man. Sue me, he was attractive. Younger than me by about ten or so years, according to his paperwork. Something I probably should keep in mind when I was ogling his backside while pretending to be pinching off the early pepper plants. He stared at me in confusion. "You don't need to beat the dirt into submission. This isn't hockey."

"You wanted it worked. It's worked." He paused to lean on the hoe, hair plastered to his head.

"True, I did, but you're exerting yourself needlessly. May I?" I motioned to the hoe. He passed it over, then used his tee as a towel for his face. My eyeballs dropped to his abs. They were nice abs, firm, with a treasure trail of copper hair that led wandering eyes to places they should not wander. I grabbed the hoe from him with more sass than I should have, my gaze flying to the soil he'd been whacking at. "Okay, so this is a Dutch hoe—"

"I dated one of those once."

I rolled my eyes, then caught a slight twitch at the corner of his mouth. "Her name is Anika."

"You've spent too much time sniffing herbicides," he tossed out. That did make me smile.

"Now, you have to be kind to ladies, as well as to your back. The handle is long enough that you don't have to bend over, or as in your case, lift it over your head as if it were a battle axe and you a mighty Viking about to behead an enemy."

He quirked one eyebrow. A bee buzzed by, stopping just for a moment to rest her tiny heinie on my shoulder. He drew back, eyes wide, and lifted his hand.

"No," I said as the honeybee sat there chilling. "We don't swat bees here in the garden. Bees are our friends. They pollinate the plants and make us yummy honey to pour into our tea."

"Yeah, they also sting."

"Only in self-defense. Are you allergic?" I didn't recall seeing that listed on his paperwork. He shook his sodden head. "Good, okay, so then there's no need to freak out if one of the girls lands on you. Just give her time to catch her tiny bee breath, try not to pinch her, and just go about with your work." The bee took to the air. "Nice to see you again, Veronica!"

"You name the bees?"

"Of course. You have a name, right?"

"Not much of one anymore," he mumbled, and I felt a sting, but not from any bee, it was a sting of sympathy. This man, for all his bitterness, was hurting. I knew how that felt. I was aware of how hard it was to pry the talons of addiction from your flesh. "Are you some sort of hippie?"

That last comment did make me laugh. "In some ways, I suppose. I've walked an incredibly rocky road. I discovered, as I stumbled and fell face down, that the earth is always willing to catch you, give you succor, and replenish what humanity and your own faults strip from you."

"Oh yeah, total hippie. I bet you did Woodstock," he said, although I saw in his lovely eyes that he was being a wiseass. Or so I assumed.

"Yep, I played backup for Jimi Hendrix." That one made him gape. "I'm kidding. Shit, I'm not *that* old."

"If I call you old, does that negate any time worked?"

"It should, but no, of course not. Now pay attention, Mike, for this is valuable information that will save your back."

He sneered at the use of a nickname. I had to wonder if he thought that would set me back on my heels. If he did, he was in for a rude awakening. I'd had tougher, more dangerous sorts come through my garden to work off service time than one pissy hockey player. I'd been the one to teach Jimmy "The Hippo" Jenkins to grow his own herbs. If I could handle "The Hippo," I could handle Michael Zhang.

Michael got bored after a single demonstration, so I handed the hoe back to him, stood back with arms folded over my chest, and watched as he worked the soil with less aggression.

"Nicely done," I said and got a nod. "It's quitting time. Feel free to linger if you want to help clean up or—"

"Later." He shoved the hoe at me, spun on his heel, and off he went.

"Yeah, I figured that was how that would go, Anika," I sighed, then rested my chin on the dirty hoe. Michael

Zhang was way past just nice from the back. His front was pretty good too. "Ugh, okay, enough lusting after the volunteers. Come on, Anika, I'll waltz you back to the tool shed."

And we danced our way to the storage shed. I spent some time walking through the plots after plant visiting hours were over for the day, taking stock of things, eyeballing the growing plants for any signs of problematic insects or blight. The sounds of the city were everywhere, all around, and yet, when I was here among the veggies and fruit trees, the din seemed lessened.

Someone had chopped a branch from a lemon tree —it sat all sad and lonely on the ground, and I glanced around as if the perpetrator was hiding in the bushes. Some people came here for their mental health, anger issues, or searching for calm, and somehow the poor lemon tree had likely taken the brunt of someone's bad day. I carried it to the composting area, turning it this way and that, wondering if I could use it for something —a wind chime or something. There were markings scored into the branch, a rough *S* and two *O*'s. I couldn't recall anyone with the initials S O O in the gardens, but my memory was not encyclopedic, and it probably meant nothing at all.

I hated waste almost as much as I resented vandalism, however upset a person was when they committed the act.

I hated having to leave this beautiful place.

I'd live here if I could, but the city zoning didn't allow a dwelling, so I had to force myself to go to my little apartment every night. I could stretch out going home though. That empty space was depressing. I moved back into the office, then after one final trip through our new greenhouse, a gift from a kilted benefactor who asked to remain nameless, but was well known in the rock community, I resigned myself to going home.

After locking the gate, I meandered down the gritty streets, stopping to visit with Bohdan until he too, was locking up, and then, made my way home. Mrs. Cho was watching *Matlock* as I passed her doorway. She did love that charming Southern lawyer. I climbed the stairs, unlocked the several locks, and stepped inside. My place was nothing grand, for sure, but it was mine. Well, I rented it, so technically, it was Mrs. Cho's, but for all intents and purposes, it was mine. It was small, filled with what made me happy, such as plants and my first guitar and pictures of Leo and me. I'd packed away the images of Courtney and me when the divorce decree was finalized. There was no point in keeping reminders of what could have been lying around. I'd made my choice. I'd chosen drugs over my family. And yes, I knew enough about addiction now that I shouldn't be saying such things about myself. I would never say it about anyone else battling for sobriety.

Somedays, it was hard to not blame myself for it all

when it had been me who had lied, stolen, and robbed Peter to pay Paul for the drugs. Courtney had tried her best to be supportive, but, in the end, she simply couldn't do it, and that was fair. With her brother's help, she and Jack had taken Leo away from the mess that was me, gotten a new place, and started over. I didn't hold a single thing against her for that decision. Hell, if I'd been living with my sorry ass through my using days, I would have left me too. I was a shitty person doing shitty things.

"Oh man," I sighed aloud, toeing off my sneakers, then padding into the kitchenette to cook up something tasty. Maybe eating would lift this post-Leo call funk I always fell into. A normal person would be happy to have spoken to his child, but I always seemed to get blue after our weekly calls. It was tough to sit here alone, with only my wok and my love of old movies to keep me company night after night. "Okay, so we stir up something yummy and check out the classic movie offerings."

I said this to my houseplants. They all seemed to agree with the plans for the night, so after whipping up a rather tasty chicken stir fry served over brown rice, I flopped down on my saggy sofa, found the remote, and flipped while I ate. I settled on an old war movie called *Tora! Tora! Tora!* starring Jason Robards, one of my favorites from ye olden days.

And so ended another day in the life of Bryce

Kincaid. Oh, the glamour. To think, if I'd stepped right, instead of left, that night in Seattle, my life might be different. Maybe, I'd still have my son living with me. Maybe, I'd be rich. Maybe, I'd be living in the hills like our kilted benefactor.

I sighed over my forkful of rice and fresh veggies.

Maybe. Maybe. Maybe.

To quote CA Fletcher, "the thing about maybes is that you can get lost in them and end up going nowhere."

I didn't want to go nowhere. I wanted to go somewhere. I *was* going somewhere. Okay, so it was a different somewhere from where I'd been heading fifteen years ago but that was *perfectly fine*. As long as I was walking that new direction clean.

THE FOLLOWING SUNDAY DAWNED BRIGHT, DRY, AND FAR too early. I'd come awake after a disturbing dream—or a replay I supposed—of one of my more disastrous days. Shaking off the memory of the day I'd come home to find a notice of tax sale for failure to pay the property taxes attached to the front door of my house, I rolled out of bed, wishing like hell the weekly meeting would have taken place this morning. That would have to wait until Wednesday evening at the local Methodist church. I could call my sponsor, but Wilt was probably sound asleep by his wife. Besides, it was a dream. Just another way for my brain to dredge up some of those blues that liked to sneak in to pull my soul down.

I showered, dressed casually, grabbed my guitar, and shuffled off to the garden. There was no sound from Mrs. Cho's when I passed her door, although Lefty was sitting in her window staring down at me. I waved at the cat, enjoying the somewhat quiet quality of a sleepy Sunday morning in the city. Traffic was light at six a.m., not nonexistent, but light. Bohdan's shop was closed today, he being a religious man, so I stopped at a small coffee/donut shop owned by a Middle Eastern couple who made the best matcha green tea in the state.

And they opened at the crack of dawn, which worked well for me when I had my bad nights. Ten minutes later, I was seated inside the garden—the gate unlocked, but closed, as we didn't open on Sundays until 1 p.m. I plunked my backside down about ten feet from the bright-colored hives, my butt on my lilac yoga mat, and pulled my beat-up six-string from my back. I ran my fingers over the strings, sighing at the gentle sounds flowing from the instrument.

Folding my legs crisscross applesauce, I began plucking away, letting the music take me where it wished me to go. That morning, it seemed to be Cat Stevens—or Yusuf Islam as he is now known—a performer who sits on my personal faves list with a few other exalted folksy types, such as James Taylor, Gordon Lightfoot, and The Lumineers.

45

I found myself singing "The Wind" as the sun began to crawl a bit higher. The creak of the garden gate pulled me from the soft, mystical place the earth and music always took me, my eyes widening to see Michael Zhang standing ten feet from me. He looked stunned.

I placed my hand over the strings as I gazed up at him. He appeared unsettled for some reason. Unsettled, but lovely. And yes, men could be lovely, especially this one with the hint of a new day on his face.

"What brings you here on a day off?" I enquired as he took a lone step closer.

"I didn't know you sang," he answered instead of addressing the statement I'd made. I noted that he did that quite a bit, deflecting, and while it might piss off people who hadn't walked the path of recovery, I saw it for what it was. Addicts are masters of deflection.

"I do a bit."

"That sounded like more than a bit." He drew closer, sharp eyes on the hives before stopping about two feet from where I sat. "You're pretty good."

"Meh," I teased, then rested my right arm atop my beloved Martin acoustic. My voice was part of a sour past. "Are you coming home from a night out?"

"No," he snapped, his face tightening. "I'm not some boozehound who drinks his way through life."

"Good," I replied, then motioned for him to sit. He balked. "The bees are sluggish right now, so they shouldn't venture too far from the hives just yet." His apprehension was obvious. I patted my yoga mat, then scooched over, curious to discover what had led him here when he could be lying abed in the lap of luxury somewhere with a curvy lady, or buff man. We'd not discussed his sexuality, nor would we. Who the man bedded had no impact at all on how well he could weed beets.

"What about wasps?" He looked around with suspicion, and winced as a bee bumbled his way.

"I call them Jack," I deadpanned.

"Jack?"

"Stinging, nasty, grumbling, pointed, ergo my ex brother-in-law Jackson. Never mind, come and rest—you look as if you could use some time to settle."

I was shocked when he did as asked, folding those long strong legs under him to sit beside me, his gaze darting to me, then the hives, then to the vegetable plots.

I strummed slowly, not playing any one song, just picking bits of this and that as he unwound.

"So, did you ride the bus here?" I asked after five minutes of us sitting side-by-side as the local flock of wild parakeets started to arrive. The tiny green birds were quite a nuisance in the garden, so we were trying different things to drive them off. So far, as evidenced by a few of them perched atop a fake owl on a post, little had worked. I waved my hand at the birds, and they took off. For now.

"You don't like birds?" Michael asked, once more skirting my question.

"I love birds, but those little stinkers have learned to pluck our peas, so we're trying a few tactics to keep them out. Fake owls is not working."

"Nope, they just shit on his head," he pointed out.

"That they did. Would you like some green tea? It's probably cool enough to sip now," I waved a hand at my takeout, then began playing the song I'd been singing when he'd arrived, sans vocals for now.

"No, I'm good. Charles stopped at a Starbucks on the way here." He stretched his legs out, leaned back on his locked arms, and stared up at the pink sky. "My brother is going to be gone for two days on a road trip to Tucson. I should be with him." Ah. Okay, well that was a bit of truth. I continued playing, letting him sort out what he wanted to say, if anything. "We had a fight."

"I'm sorry that you two fought," I offered, playing on, my gaze flitting to Michael's profile time and again.

"We always do," he whispered to the sky, his eyes closing slowly.

"Have you thought about not arguing with him?" I said.

"I'm not the one who starts them."

I said nothing more, simply sat and played, grateful for his troubled and prickly company. While I cherished my time here alone on our little two acres of happy veggies, sometimes I worried my rambling conversations with honey bees might suggest I required more human interaction. And no one seemed more human or more in need of something than Michael Zhang did right now, so I played on. He stared at the sky, and it was what it needed to be. Sometimes, that was all one could ask of a morning.

Chapter 5

Michael

MY RESTLESSNESS DROVE ME OUT FOR AN EARLY RUN, but it was just my fucking luck that I met Charles loading stuff into his car, ready to head out to the team jet and off to Vancouver for an away game. I thought about turning back—the last thing I needed was him lecturing me over some perceived infraction of his moral code—but it was too late, because tripping over his sticks meant he must have heard me, as well as seen me.

"Good morning," he said with such a bright tone it set my teeth on edge. Bryce's comment on maybe not arguing with my brother spun in my thoughts, but Charles was in his suit, all dressed up, ready for the flight, and I was done.

"Is it? Not for me it isn't because I'm not the one flying up to Vancouver." I couldn't keep the edge out of my voice, couldn't mask my jealousy and anger, and bitterness coated my words. "Must be nice, still getting to play."

Charles, loading his gear, paused. "You want to do this now?" he asked, and turned to face me, and fuck, he looked way more tired than normal.

"Do what? Rail at the fucking heavens that the assholes took my career away from me."

"You did that to yourself," he murmured.

"Fuck you," I snarled, and his shoulders hunched.

"How's the therapy going?"

Had he *really* gone there? "And fuck that as well," I snarled, temper and grief were an evil mix in my chest.

"It's just, I was doing some reading, and thought… look… have you considered trying Gamblers Anonymous?"

"No," I snapped, hating the idea of strangers poking into my life. "I don't need a bunch of people in my business."

"Then, do you want to talk to me?" He sounded hopeful, but the last thing I wanted was to talk about anything with Charles, unless it was about sticks and pucks. I didn't answer, just huffed an incredulous laugh. "I care," he pointed out. "I've done everything I can to—"

"I didn't ask you to play savior," I retorted, the bitterness evident. He'd paid for the lawyers and the therapy; I lived in his pool house for nothing; I didn't want anything else from him.

"I'm your brother, and I'm just trying to help," he

said, and even took a step closer, his hand outstretched as if he wanted to hug me or something. Nope. Not happening.

"We're not real brothers," I said. The words tasted awful, and I regretted them instantly, but pride kept me silent, the weight of our shared, yet divided, history hanging heavy in the air. The Zhang family may well have adopted me, but that didn't mean Charles was my blood. No, somewhere out there was my real family, and yeah, I'd never wanted to find them, but I sometimes wondered if whoever had left me could have made sense of my world. They might even see that none of what had happened to me in the last year was my fault.

Charles stumbled back as if I'd hit him, but composed himself, tipping his chin. "You've been my brother since our parents adopted you. So, I'm here for you, for whatever you need, regardless."

I turned away then, the weight of our shared past and my own anxiety and anger too heavy to confront in the cold light of dawn. "You're not helping when all you're doing is doling out charity," I retorted, my voice rising. "I don't need it!"

Charles's expression softened. "But you do."

"I could really hate you," I snapped.

He shrugged then. "And I will *always* love you, Michael."

I grumbled as I headed inside, picked up the mail on

the mat, marketing flyers, and an envelope with my address and name, but no identifying marks.

My heart stopped.

Not another one.

500. Every Day. 500 more.

And worse, right on its heels, there was a recording. I placed the phone to my ear and pressed play.

My voice, but these couldn't be my words tinged with desperation begging for just twenty k more.

And saying in no uncertain terms, I'd throw a game against Boston.

I deleted it straight away—what if the team heard that, what if Charles heard it?

I would never do that. I couldn't…

But that was clearly me on the jumpy recording, and I sounded drunk.

And desperate.

———

ANOTHER WEEK INTO THE GRIND, AND I WAS NOWHERE near "finding myself" or whatever enlightenment the court promised would come from manual labor. The recording was just a blur in my head, another nail in my coffin as each day here was a tedious marathon, stretching my patience thin. Every morning, I'd drag myself out of the pool house, to whatever car service Charles had organized for me in his absence, waiting to take me for my community service. The dirt under my nails mocked me, a reminder I was grounded—literally. The repetition of planting, watering, digging, was monotonous. The sun wasn't invigorating, it was hot; and the earth wasn't nurturing, it was dirty. Not to mention people kept wanting to talk to me, ask me questions about whatever green thing I was planting, and I didn't want to talk to people. I missed the ice, the cold clarity of the rink. Out here, in the dirt and the sweat, I felt like a stranger to myself.

Take this thing I had in my hand—leafy green-ness, check; roots trapped in a pot, check; some weird-ass Latin name, check; Bryce hovering next to me in case I killed his precious baby… triple check. The plant was one of those abandoned things that had been donated to the garden, way past a seedling and pot-bound, and Bryce was getting me to rescue a whole wheelbarrow of thirty of them. If I had to take a guess, it was some kind of lesson for me so I could feel some connection to Mother Earth blah blah.

Or it was a whole rescue-a-plant-rescue-me thing.

"You don't have to watch me," I said.

He didn't move, and when I glanced his way, he had that annoying eyebrow thing going on.

"I do," he said, and that was it, no explanation about why he had to watch me, or whether I was doing right or wrong, just that simple two-word answer that was infuriating.

"What do you think I'm going to do? Stamp on it?"

His eyebrow lifted a hair higher. "Are you going to stamp on it?"

"What? No, of course not. I'm not doing time for being a serial stamper." I was disgruntled, but I swear his mouth twitched then. "Are you laughing at me?" I hated being laughed at, or as Therapist Three put it, my aversion to criticism was linked to issues with self-esteem. Her words not mine.

I hate that she even thought I didn't have self-esteem—I was a goddamn NHL star for fuck's sake.

Anyway, no one likes to be laughed at, and no one wants to be criticized for messing up.

"It's just this image of a big bad hip-checking hockey player stamping on a teeny tiny Capsicum annuum."

I huffed at his use of the Latin name, when he could have just called it by what it was—a goddamn bell pepper. How did he make these Latin words sound so sexy?

Shit, I needed to get laid.

Ignoring Bryce, I teased out the roots all cramped in the pot, before laying the baby with care on one palm. "Maybe it deserved to be stamped on. Maybe this innocent-looking whatever-it's-called is actually the kind of bell pepper that bullies all the other plants." I was joking, and god knows where that came from, but Bryce read something into the words, as he was prone to do.

"So, bullies should be stamped into the ground?" he summarized.

"I didn't say that."

"Physical violence is never the answer," Bryce observed.

I swear I was this close to shoving the plant in his face. Only I didn't, because I was the bigger man, and I didn't resort to violence unless I was strapped to skates and needed to get the team a win.

"Woo Woo hippy McDrippy," I muttered as he sauntered off. How could anyone so sexy be so self-righteous. I bet he'd never known a day's bad luck in his entire life.

I went to a crouch, widening the hole the chili plant would go into. I followed everything I'd been told, burying it up to the base of its stem and watering it, and then, I glanced around me to see if any well-meaning gardeners were in the vicinity.

I was alone, I patted the tiny plant. "Grow big."

Then, with a sigh, I moved onto the next one.

THE CAR SERVICE DROPPED ME AT THE SIDE GATE WITH the code—no front gate for me—and I headed past the main house and through the expansive yard to the pool house. It was more of a garden room with wooden siding and was hot, plus it was at the opposite side of the yard to the pool, so yeah, weird name.

But it was home, and I fumbled the key, then

juggled dinner—Pringles—and locked myself inside. The athlete in me cried that I wasn't sitting down to protein and vegetables, the stubborn ass in me was all for eating the entire tube of Pringles, and I knew I'd have work to do getting back to fitness for next season.

After all, I had no doubt a team out there would want me for my skill with a stick, rather than my lack of skill in poker games.

I sent off a quick text to Petra, agent extraordinaire, or rather ex-agent extraordinaire.

Michael: And?

The answer was quick, and the same as it had been since she'd dropped me.

Petra: Not your agent. Go away.

My thought was that if I kept the lines of communication open, she would ignore the fact she'd left me and throw me a bone. After all, what agent would turn down ten percent of my next contract?

My big contract. Millions.

Maybe not with the Storm, but with someone.

I need to pay off Loopy for that recording. I rubbed my chest where it hurt—I didn't remember saying any of that, so it must be someone else.

Nothing can fucking hurt me because I am Michael *freaking* Zhang.

"Okay, let's do this," I said to the empty room, because that was what an idiot did when faced with silence—he talked to himself.

The game buildup started, the Storm playing in

Vancouver, and I scrolled my phone, opening the app store and finding my favorite betting app. I'd deleted them all because Therapist One said they were bad for me, backed up by Therapist Two, and thirded by Therapist Three. But, what would it hurt to download the app and create a new account. I didn't have a lot of money, all my credit cards were gone, my accounts all tied up with the agency that Charles had brought in to monitor what was left of my money.

Fucking Charles.

I still had a small allowance, a hundred dollars or so for emergencies, and this was a sure thing, right? The Storm was the better team, and even without me, they were going to win.

Just ten dollars.

The addiction that had brought me so low was whispering promises of even greater highs, and fuck me, I was all too willing to listen.

I SIGNED UP TO A NEW EMAIL ACCOUNT JUST TO USE ON the app, then stalled at the first hurdle. I had to top up the betting account. That would mean money leaving my emergency fund, which Charles had access to, because of course he did.

Fuck him.

I paid in fifty dollars, placed the bet, and shoved my phone under a cushion. The odds were okay, I'd placed everything on the Storm to win, and I could almost taste the high of victory when I tripled those fifty dollars.

Charles couldn't comment that I was wasting money if I was making money.

Only, I forced myself to forget about the bet when the Storm was three goals down by the end of the first period, and instead, focused on the camera close-ups of my brother. I could see Charles was fuming as he led the team off the ice, incandescent with rage, and I could almost taste the anger they'd be getting the brunt of when the locker room door shut. The Storm looked beaten, chagrined, shadows of themselves, and for a brief moment, I felt vindicated. Seeing them trail behind, floundering against Vancouver's onslaught, I felt a twisted sense of satisfaction. For years, I'd been part of their strength, and there was a part of me that felt justified in their loss without me being there—the same as every other time I'd watched them lose in the last three months.

My second therapist said this was a way of coping with feelings of displacement and concluded that it showed I had underlying issues of self-worth or a need for acknowledgment. My first therapist had said pretty much the same thing.

My third therapist—the current one, who'd been forced to take me on because it was mandated by the court—suggested it was deeper than that, and for a moment, I'd felt happy that she'd seen through Therapist One and Two's bullshit. Then, she'd ruined it all today by suggesting it likely tied to abandonment issues from being thrown away as a baby, and maybe, we should unpick my feelings about being adopted by the Zhang family.

Nope.

Not doing that.

I needed to find a therapist who saw the *real* me.

The unlucky me who didn't deserve any of this shit.

Meanwhile, the Storm were struggling, and my absence had been noticed by the pundits who'd dissected the plays so far, deemed them abysmal, and then, launched into how much the team needed me.

Erik Solberg leaned into the microphone, his voice carrying the distinctive melody of his Norwegian roots. "You can't deny they've been off their rhythm without Michael Zhang," he said, his analysis sharp and concise.

Liam Tremblay, fellow pundit, and someone who'd never broken into the NHL, nodded. "Yeah, Zeetoo isn't just a second liner; he was the backbone on that right wing."

"Stop calling me Zeetoo," I mumbled at the screen. When I was growing up as Charles's younger brother, the hockey nickname—the second Zhang brother, Zhang-as-well—became Zeetoo. Where others thought this was cute, I saw the "too" part as two, the second in freaking everything. Still, nicknames stuck, and that one would follow me until the end of my natural life.

Or my hockey life anyway.

Erik was still talking, "… his absence is felt. The second line's just not generating the same pressure. They need his aggression and playmaking ability."

The conversation drifted to my suspension, the elephant in the room. "Do you think we'll see him return?" Liam mused, casting a speculative glance at Erik, who leaned forward in his chair as if he was about to share the best kind of gossip.

"It's a tough one. Zhang's suspension has hit the Storm hard. More so given he's the captain's brother, but coming back? Talent's there, no question, but the severity of what he did, and how he let everyone down… word is that there's no way back for him. I can't see he will—"

I switched the channel.

What do commentators know about anything, anyway?

My cell vibrated, and I pulled it out from its hiding place to check the screen. Unknown Text, but I opened it, because I always did.

500. And 500 more. Every day. Just say yes.

I threw the cell back to the cushions—I didn't want to break the only way I could follow the results of the bet—and ignored the pointed message.

Loopy was reminding me that the money to pay for his silence was increasing by five hundred dollars a day.

Not a week. A day.

I buried the fear again, the adrenaline of the gamble

on the win was enough for me to forget the text, even more so, when I deleted it.

I made a coffee, opened the tube of Pringles, and headed back to the TV, catching a shitload of ads for new cars, and then, watched the teams come back out on the ice.

The grainy screen did little to contain my frustration as I continued to watch the Storm flounder.

"Come on! What was that pass?" I shouted, my voice ricocheting off the pool house walls. I was on my feet now, every fiber of my being wanting to be on that ice, correcting the mistakes, rallying the team. When Prez missed what should have been an easy shot, my hand collided with the wall. "Jesus! You're better than this!" I yelled, as if they could hear me after each missed opportunity, but I was powerless to stop it.

As the third period started, the Storm looked like a different team, but so did Vancouver, relentless in their offense. "Defense! Watch the—No!" I groaned, the Storm's defense faltering, leaving Pageau to fend for himself. The screen flickered as if sympathizing with my agitation.

"Skate, Ashman, skate!" I found myself coaching from the couch, leaping to my feet with every close call. When the camera panned to my brother's face, his expression was flat. I knew that expression—Charles could sense a loss, and if the captain knew the game was done, then what were the rest of the team gonna do?

They wouldn't rally around a captain who acted as if he'd given up.

Where was Charles's temper? Where was his fire?

Two minutes left, and the Storm had clawed back enough to level at three goals each. "That's it! Yes!" I could taste my win—the team's win—and I cheered, hands raised in triumph with each score. But as the buzzer signaled the end of regulation time, I sank back, the high of the comeback marred by the bitter taste of what was to come.

Overtime was a knife-edge, and the Storm seemed blunted. My shouts grew hoarser, urging them on through the screen, but the final goal from Prez, stopped from Vancouver was a punch to the gut.

I turned off the TV, the silence pressing in.

I'd lost the fifty dollars.

RESTLESS, I HEADED INTO THE GARDEN, THE VAST SPACE filled with scrubby bushes and, near the house, kid's toys, and a big wooden climbing frame. I walked the balance bar, jumping off the end to land in a superhero pose. "And the crowd roars!" I sketched a bow and chuckled.

"I wish you weren't here," a voice said from behind me.

I whirled around to face my sister-in-law, Clare.

She was leaning against the patio door, her expression cold in the flood of the security light. "I wish you weren't staying in the pool house, Michael. It's… wrong." She and I had never seen eye to eye over things—she kept wanting me at family events, but what single guy wanted to eat birthday cake and pretend to have fun? Maybe one day, I'd settle down to it, but not when I was still in my twenties.

I shrugged, trying to mask the sting of her words. "I don't exactly love the arrangement either, Clare. But it's temporary."

"Temporary or not, Charles hates it!"

My heart cracked at that. He'd been the one to suggest I stay. "It was Charles's idea—"

"I heard the two of you, fighting, and he doesn't deserve that in his life."

"He doesn't understand—"

"He'd do anything for you, Michael, and you throw it back in his face every single time."

"That's not fair—"

"You being here disrupts our family and upsets the kids," she added, her voice sharp.

That was news to me—I hadn't even seen my nieces to upset them. "I don't spend time with your kids," I retorted, and it was clear that was the wrong thing to say.

"*My* kids?" she said, incredulous, "they're not just *my* kids. They're *your* nieces, and *you* haven't spoken to them since you moved in."

"See! How could I have upset them, then!"

"By not giving a shit about them, or their father!" Clare yelled.

"Momma?"

Clare froze in horror and turned to see a very awake Hope, the oldest of my nieces at just over four. I think. Or five? Maybe six? She was way small. I knew Grace was two years younger than her, but that didn't help me to figure it out.

She was wearing princess PJs, and with her tousled dark curls and half-awake grumble, she reminded me of a miniature version of her dad, and as I started to back away, not sure how to act, Clare scooped her up.

"Uncle Red!" Hope called, snuggling against her mom while fixing her sleepy gaze on me. Uncle Michael was too much of a mouthful and had somehow become Red for my hair, which fascinated her. I'd always made sure the birthday cards I sent them, with a generous amount of money inside, of course, had something red on the front.

Kind of an in-joke between uncle and nieces. Right?

I swallowed hard, managing a soft "Hiya, Hope," while trying to channel my best Uncle voice—the one free of curses and anger, the one that wouldn't upset anyone.

And then, before she could need me for anything, I gave a half wave and hurried back to the pool house.

I had essential things to do, like come up with a reason why I'd put fifty dollars onto an app, and then lost the lot.

But more importantly, I had Pringles to finish.

Chapter 6

Bryce

The holiday weekend was four days away. Gardeners were flowing in and out, hurrying to tend to their plots before they left for wherever it was they were headed to. I'd managed to gather up several boxes of veggies with the help of a local Chippy Chipmunks scout group when I got a call. Ignoring the buzzing in my back pocket as I supervised Michael carrying crates of produce to the back of a Subaru Forester belonging to one of the scout moms—a lovely lady named Penny, who made a point of telling me she was very serious about gardens and gardeners on more than one occasion—my butt wouldn't stop vibrating.

I pulled my phone out, irked that someone was tugging me from one of the most enjoyable aspects of my day the past few weeks: watching Michael Zhang work. When I saw it was Courtney ringing, I got a rush of several emotions, concern leading the way. I'd only spoken to Leo yesterday, and all had seemed fine, other than he was not happy about the Yellowstone trip all of a sudden. I'd tried to play it up even though it had killed me to do so, but he'd seemed reluctant.

"I'll be in the office. Thank you girls, and gardeners!" I shouted to the folks milling about. The plot renters all replied with waves of dirty hands. The girls in the brown uniforms made chipmunk squeaks. They were too cute. Michael threw me a look over his shoulder as he toted a box of spuds to the SUV. The veggies would be taken to a nearby shelter. I tapped the green button on my cell as soon as I skidded into my office.

"Hey," I panted into the phone, easing the door closed just a bit with my butt. "Is everything okay?"

"Not really," my ex sighed. "And Leo is fine health-wise, so stop worrying."

"I wasn't worried." I was *totally* worried.

"Yes, you were. You have that furrow on your brow."

"I do not." I smoothed the lines away with a grimy hand.

"Liar," she snickered, then sighed once more. "Okay, so despite all of Tony's and my wheedling, it looks like Leo is now not at all interested in Yellowstone."

"Oh, yeah, he mentioned that yesterday when we video-chatted."

"Did you say something to him?"

"If you're asking if I tried to talk him out of it, no,

and I kind of resent that you would think I would undermine you in that way." I padded around my desk, ignoring the mound of paperwork that had piled up. I loved managing this garden. I loathed the office work that came with the job. But since the city could barely afford to pay me, finding someone to do the secretarial work—was it okay to use that term anymore?—well, no one was going to do this work for a few pennies a day, no matter if they could take home all the free cukes they could eat.

"Sorry, I'm just at my wit's end. We had everything planned, and now he's backing out. I hate to force him to go, and for the life of me, I do not know why he's changed his mind. He loves nature."

I turned to face the rear wall of my stuffy space. "He wouldn't say anything to me other than he didn't want to go. Maybe someone said something at school?"

"Yeah, maybe, anyway, so Tony and I are still interested in going. The hotel reservations are made, and he's got a speech prepared for the seminar. Would it be okay if Leo flew out and spent Easter break with you?"

I mouthed "YES!" then threw a fist into the air several times while shaking my ass in pure glee. "That should be fine," I replied while still shimmying in place. "Should I fly out to get him?"

"Well, that's another point. He wants to fly out alone, and Jack thinks it might be good for him."

"Your brother has no idea what… No, nope, no way."

"Bryce, he's seven now. The airlines allow kids five and up to fly unaccompanied."

"Nope, no way is my child flying alone. Not until he's at least sixteen. No, eighteen. No, twenty-one. Yes, twenty-one."

She giggled. "I feel the same way, but his friend flies alone all the time. I think he feels we're babying him, and Jack said—"

"I don't care what Jack said. Also, I have no shame in babying our son. I can grab a flight out to Arizona to get him. Or, hey, I could drive out? It's not that far."

"Are you sure you want to drive?"

"Of course. We'll make a day of it. I'll leave super early, get there around noon or close to it, and we can take our time coming home. Maybe stop at some greasy spoon for dinner so he can eat unhealthy food that his mom won't let him eat at home."

"Ugh, you creep." We both laughed. "Yeah, okay, that sounds nice. I'll let him know to be ready Saturday morning. Is that too soon?"

"Nope. Not at all. Thank you, Courtney, for not making the boy go."

"Meh, I'm disappointed, but he seems set on seeing you, and that feels more important than watching buffalo poop in the road. Also, five days kid-free with a hot forest ranger? Yes please!"

Okay, that was a mental image I did not wish to

have in my brain. While I did still care for her in that brotherly ex-husband way, I did *not* need to imagine her and Tony doing the deed.

"So, I'll see you in two days then," I rushed to change the subject.

"Yep, thanks again for being so flexible, Bryce. See you Saturday."

And just like that, my whole world seemed that much brighter.

"You got some good moves for an old gardener," Michael said from behind me, startling me so bad I bobbled my phone. Cheeks red, I spun to face him lingering in the doorway, and he was far too sexy in his tight T-shirt and cargo shorts. The man had incredible calves.

"You're never too old to play in the dirt or shake your groove thing." He stared at me with a blank expression. "It's an old disco song?" Still nothing. "Never mind. I'm in a good mood because my son is going to spend a whole week here with me."

"Oh, that's cool. I didn't know you had a kid." I waved a hand at the fifteen pictures in frames on my desk, all with snapshots of me and Leo. "Yeah, sorry, guess I didn't notice."

"Good thing they weren't bears," I teased, my head whirling with things I needed to do before Leo arrived.

"What about bears?"

"The pictures. It's a good thing they weren't bears, or you would have been eaten."

"Right." He gave me the same kind of look Leo did when I said something termed to be old and dumb. "Anyway, so the chipmunk girls got all the veggies. What do you need me to do next?"

"Oh, uhm, let's uhm… sorry, I'm kind of scattered. I wasn't planning on driving to Arizona, and now my schedule is a little up in the air."

He got this funny sort of constipated expression on his face. "You're driving to Arizona over the weekend? Where exactly?"

"Tucson," I replied. "Why?"

"Oh, nothing, just the Storm is playing in Tucson on Saturday afternoon is all. If you wanted, I could call in a favor and get you and your kid tickets to the game."

"That's incredibly kind, Michael. Thank you." To say I was flabbergasted would be an understatement. I hadn't seen much in the way of thoughtfulness for other people from Michael Zhang, something not uncommon with those battling addictions. We addicts did tend to be rather self-serving. "He'll love that. Oh turnips, I have to find a group meeting tonight, if possible. I wonder if they're having the one over in the Baptist mission early this week because of the holidays?"

He studied me like a fly he had Mr. Miyagi'd out of the air. "You have a group?"

"Yeah, NA, narcotics anonymous." I stopped flittering around on my phone looking for Chet's phone number—Chet being the head of the Skid Row chapter—to meet his confused gaze. "I'm five years clean now."

"No shit," he whispered, ignoring a honey bee that flew into the office beside him.

"No shit. I was hooked on pain killers. Kind of ruined a pretty good life that I had going. Damn that fentanyl. Don't you do a group meeting?"

That made his hackles rise. "No, why the hell would I go sit in some damp church basement and tell a bunch of losers what makes me a loser, too?"

Wow. That was a lot to unpack. "Well, for one thing, people who are in group aren't losers. I tend to feel that folks who talk about their issues, who share the struggles as well as the accomplishments, are incredibly strong. It takes courage to examine your mistakes."

He stared at me as if I'd said something outlandish. Like cucumber salad wasn't one of the best things on the face of the planet. Or that bees weren't lovely little friends. Speaking of winged friends…

"Come on, Amanda, you're not allowed to bash your face into the window. Queen Daphne needs you." I made my way to the dirty window, lifted the honeybee from the pane with infinite care, and walked her outside. "There you go." I held my finger up and the bee buzzed off toward the hives in the corner.

"You are the weirdest person I have ever met," Michael said as he walked past. Did he mean I was weird because I believed in the power of group meetings or that I spoke to insects? Not that it mattered, I was curious about what made the man tick. I watched as he picked up a hoe and went to work on Mrs. Phillips' corn patch. It did need weeding badly, but the old gal was too old to do that job herself, so our volunteers did it for her. That he had set into his work without being told what to do was a good sign. It meant he was learning what made a garden grow, other than silver bells, cockleshells, and pretty maids all in a row.

Feeling I'd perhaps given the man something to ponder on, I returned to my office to focus on paperwork—Lord help me—and plan out the very best week for a dad and his son ever in the history of dad-and-son weeks.

"DAD, DID YOU *SEE* THAT?!" LEO SHOUTED TO BE HEARD over the roars of the home crowd. Seemed hockey fans were rather rabid. Who knew? Not me. I'd never really been big into sports. Oh sure, I'd played whatever the gym teachers had made us play, but I hadn't jibed with athletics all that much. I'd much rather focus on yoga, or tai chi, with some big walks when I could fit them in. So being front and center—and I do mean front and center—for my first professional hockey game was a real eye-opener. "Did you see that big blond Raptor guy hit that big Storm guy? He knocked him off his skates! Holy crap, Dad, this is incredible!"

"It's something, that's for sure," I agreed as Michael's brother Charles, the captain of the Storm, was picking himself up off the ice about two feet in front of us. Michael had organized some great seats right beside the penalty box, and even though I'd caught one or two minutes of the insanity on the TV, it was quite the experience being this close to the glass. We'd seen players smashed into the boards eye to eye. Also, as an aside, I'd thought Michael was a behemoth in sneakers and street clothes. These guys were massive when they were on the ice with all that padding under their jerseys.

"Dad, do you think I'll be able to talk to Michael at the gardens while I'm there?" Leo glanced my way, his cheeks flushed with excitement and his chin smeared with ketchup from the second footlong hot dog he was in the process of demolishing.

I dabbed at his face with my napkin, balancing my footlong in one hand. My drink was on the floor between my feet. A trick that I'd learned right off the first time two giants in skates hit the glass and spilled the beer belonging to the guy on my left just as we'd returned for the third period. Leo took lots of pee breaks. Could be related to the enormous root beers he'd been slurping on to wash down his hot dogs.

"I should think so. He's doing volunteer work, so he'll be around." I took a bite of my hot dog, licking up the spicy mustard that got into my mustache, as the goalie for the Storm made a big save that brought sighs of frustration from the Raptor fans.

"What did he do wrong?" Leo asked. He knew that the community garden was a place for people who were working off court sentences to serve their time. Courtney and I tried to be as honest with our son as we could. He also knew I'd had some trouble with some bad pills in the past, but that I was now free of the pills. He'd been so small when Courtney had left that we'd been able to put off that difficult discussion with him until he was old enough to ask why we'd stopped being married. To be honest, I'm not sure he even recalled when we were a couple, he was barely two when she had reached her limits. So, him asking about Michael was common, he did that quite often.

"If he wants to tell you that, then it's his call," I reminded him gently. "But don't pressure him into talking about it. Lots of people who had troublesome pasts aren't in good places to be talking about it like me and your mom are, so that's—Holy cowbells!" I shouted when the Storm scored a goal out of the blue. Probably, it wasn't unexpected at all, I'd just been talking to my boy and lost track of the game. "Hey, that's Charles who scored!"

We both cheered the Storm. The Raptor fan to my left leveled an accusatory glance my way, then took a loud slurp of his newest beer. Leo and I shared a look, giggled, and dove back into our wieners, which were quite tasty. I hoped eating something filled with so many nitrates wouldn't set off a headache. They did that to me on occasion, but I'd deal. Spending this time with Leo here at the game was worth a headache. He was having a blast.

"Hey, buddy, when you do see Michael, make sure you thank him for the seats, okay?" I nudged him in the side. He glanced at me, cheeks full of hot dog, and nodded. I chuckled, rubbed the chipmunk-cheeked boy's hair, and sat back to enjoy the rest of our hockey matinee. All thanks to Michael. I'd have to think of some way to pay him back for this treat. Maybe I could make him a dish of cucumber salad.

Everyone loved my cucumber salad because I used Mrs. Cho's recipe. No one I had ever served it to had said they didn't like it, so I was sure Michael would love it.

Chapter 7

Michael

I'D BEEN QUIET IN THIS LATEST THERAPY SESSION, WHERE on a normal day I was defensive and argumentative, this time, I was dealing with an overwhelming feeling of dread, thoughts swirling about Charles finding out about the bet.

And worse, hearing that recording and hating me forever.

The Storm was due back later today, and so far, I'd been able to forget what I'd done and had pushed it into the deal-with-it-when-it-happens category. He was relentless in messaging me, checking in, every message the same tone, the same question about how I was doing, just worded in different ways. It helped that the messages hadn't blipped after the game, but I knew he must have seen what I'd done, given he co-owned the damn pocket money account he'd set up. I was heading for a lecture when he got home, but worse, he would give me that look—the one that said he was disappointed, but not surprised.

He was disappointed, but not surprised the time I drove a baseball through Dad's new television when I was nine.

Or when I skipped school every frozen day to skate.

Or when I made Mom cry.

Or the time I was at All-Star with him in Vegas and vanished for twenty-four hours.

Always disappointed, but never surprised.

I could almost hear the speech he'd give me, each word a reminder of how far I'd strayed from what I should have been doing and the dread inside me was overwhelming. It wasn't only the fear of getting caught; it was knowing that, once again, I'd let my brother down. And in his house, under his roof, that feeling of guilt was amplified.

And all of that flooded me even as Essie Laurier—therapist, hardass, focused, intense—stared at me. We'd completed the pleasantries, and she'd gone straight for the jugular.

"Can I take you back to when you were five?"

Please don't.

I wished she'd smile, because then I could smile back and work the room. I was good at that—had people eating from my hands with my charm—only she didn't give any quarter, and so I was left bare and hurting, with no defense.

"I'm not sure what being five has to do with any of this."

She pursed her lips in disapproval. Part of our chats was her getting me to accept things that weren't true—like the fact that my self-esteem issues started way *way* back.

I didn't have self-esteem issues.

I was Michael freaking Zhang, for fuck's sake. Millionaire hockey player.

Well, ex-millionaire.

For now.

"At five years old, you were adopted by Monica and Owen Zhang, who had a son, Charles, aged eight."

I rolled my eyes and settled back in the chair. "I don't remember much about all of that," I lied.

I remembered it all. It was a blur of emotions and faces. I know I'd felt uprooted because there was this woman called Sue, who gave me cookies and goodnight kisses, yet I remembered the kind of hope a kid gets on Christmas Eve, one of getting a new family to love me. I remembered Charles, wearing a hockey jersey, giving me a kiddie-stick, telling me he was going to be the best big brother. I remembered the big house, a new mom and dad, and it being warm. I'd always felt a tiny bit like an outsider, trying to fit into a puzzle where the pieces weren't quite shaped for me, knew I had to try hard to be good in case they sent me back. Of course, they never would have done that because the love was there, but so was the constant, subtle awareness of my different start in life.

"Tell me one thing you do remember," Essie said, and I thought about what part of all that I was happy to tell her. Something that wouldn't have her jumping down my throat and announcing this was why I was an addict.

"Charles gave me a hockey stick." I moved my hands into position as if I were holding that memory now. "One of those kids' ones."

"Is that where you got your love of hockey?"

"Sure, let's go with that," I said, then sighed when she lifted an eyebrow. "My love of hockey was that stick, yeah, but also the way Charles loved the game, the way our parents schlepped him to practices, and then me, because I'd become addicted to the ice, to the skating, to wanting to feel the same thing Charles felt that made him smile so hard. I wanted to smile that hard. I wanted to love something that much."

"Do you love hockey?" she asked after a pause.

I felt shaky at the words I'd just used, and it took me a moment to understand what she asked. "Sure."

"That's a strange word to use."

"It's a word," I deadpanned.

"It's a small word for a man to use who used to play a professional game for a living."

"There's no used to," I snapped. "I'll get it back."

"Sure," she said, and it was easy to see what she'd

done. That simple word held an entire book full of other things that weren't said.

"Sure?"

"Sure."

I held back the curse word threatening to trip off my tongue. "I love hockey, okay?"

"Do you?"

"I just said so."

"What do you love about hockey?"

Oh, for fuck's sake. "The fights, the adrenaline, the goals, the crowd, traveling with the team, the friends…"

The friends? Yeah, well they hadn't been around recently. Cameron was off getting married and being happy, Prez was avoiding me, or I was avoiding him, and Charles was being a goddamned saint and controlling my fucking life.

I felt antsy, wound up, stressed.

"Can you close your eyes for me?" she asked.

"Why?" My hands were fists in my lap, and I was ready to run. I didn't want to close my damn eyes.

"Close your eyes, Michael."

I did what she asked, and I could feel how my scowl was screwing up my face.

"Tell me how it feels when you take that first step onto the ice?"

"Is it a game night?" I asked and opened my eyes to see her shrug.

"Is that part important?" she said, and I wanted to

get up out of my chair and… fuck knows what… storm out probably. "Close your eyes, Michael, and tell me."

"Okay, it's a game night, we've done the warmups, and this is for the game, no wait… I wouldn't be on the fucking ice, my line is never first out, I'm always second…" My chest hurt, and I pressed a fist against the pain.

"Breathe, Michael."

If one more person tells me to breathe…

After a few moments in which I tried my hardest to freaking breathe, I thought back to the ice, but I couldn't find the words.

"Imagine the rink is empty," she encouraged.

"Ummm… so it's cold, the chill of the air is… invigorating, reminds me of winter days on the back pond." I bet she loved that, me giving analogies and shit.

"Okay, what do you hear?"

"The scrape of my skates against ice, and even though the rink is empty, I can imagine the roar of the crowd."

"So even on your own, you're playing to the crowd."

"No, the fuck? I'm telling you…"

"Close your eyes, Michael."

I hadn't even realized I'd opened them again, so I screwed them shut tight. "The ice is where I feel most alive, most at home. I skate in circles at first, just round and round, picking up speed until I'm going at top speed, using my stick in the curves, balancing on the blades, and I'm fast. I was fastest skater at All-Star last year, easily beat everyone, won fifty off of Tennant Rowe, but it was a sure thing..." I stopped. Yes, I was the fastest, but had I been fast because of sheer talent or because I'd been determined to win against the Railers captain? I swallowed. I didn't want to ask myself questions like that, but my brain and my mouth weren't in sync. I opened my eyes then, tears pricking at them.

"I put a bet on a game," I blurted. "And I didn't mean to."

"Okay?"

"And I don't know how to stop it."

MIDDAY SUN BEAT DOWN ON US AS BRYCE AND I WORKED in the garden, both of us in caps to shield from the glare. I didn't know what to say or do to him, or anyone, still raw from this morning's therapy session, exhausted by it all.

"And then, all you need to do is tuck it in," Bryce finished his lecture of how to bury a potato seedling 101 and glanced at me in expectation. His brown eyes were brimming with excitement that I could do this. He didn't ask why I was clattering around the potting shed pretending to search for a spade, nor how I hadn't said a word to anyone, nor why I probably looked as if I were going to cry at any minute.

The space here was six-by-six, the goal was to turn over the soil, aerate it, dig in manure, and then, bury the seedlings in rows. Everything was so regimented, so precise, and so different from how Bryce was—with his random smiles, and his quick sense of humor, which happened without planning—and I couldn't get the thought out of my head that he knew addiction.

What kind of addiction?

Did he chase the high of something to try and corral a wild impulsive nature? Why did that thought make me sad? He was a funny guy, sweet with the other gardeners, cute with kids, generous with his time… but was he ever wild? Did he ever dance naked in the pumpkin patch?

I stifled a snicker at the thought, but not before a strange snort had escaped, and he frowned at me.

"You okay?" he asked, then glanced down at the neat rows of planting as if he were searching for the joke that had made me laugh.

"You ever thought of randomly throwing the seeds, like nature might do, instead of these regimented rows? Like letting go of all the order and just letting nature do its thing?" I asked out of left field.

He chuckled in that annoying, but sexy, all-knowing way of his, then shook his head. "You can't harvest from chaos as easily as you can these rows."

"Yeah, but sometimes… don't you just want to throw caution to the wind and plant on the diagonal or something?"

"Why do you ask?" He patted in another plant.

"Because I think I can see wildness in you," I blurted, and he glanced at me, an unreadable expression in his eyes. "And you don't let it out."

He shrugged, which was a non-answer as bad as *sure*. Then, he checked his watch. "I have ten. Follow me."

Bryce led me past the shed and to the far outer ring of the gardens, right back against the wall of an old factory building that had been converted into apartments. There was a high hedge there, and a tall gate overgrown with a plant winding its way through the metal. He frowned at something to our left, and I followed his glance, but didn't catch what the words he scuffed away from the wood said. He mumbled something about the initials *SOO*, pushed back a loose piece of lumber, then brightened as he unlocked the gate, eased it open gently, and gestured for me to go through.

"It's a secret garden?" I asked, recalling a distant memory of a film about this kind of thing, or a book, or something. I was hit by a wave of wildflowers, an array of colors that made me blink, and the air was alive with the hum of bees.

Bryce's eyes lit up as we stepped into the chaos of

vibrant life, a stark contrast to the structured rows of the main garden.

He eased the gate shut behind us. "This," he said with a hint of pride, "is what happens when nature takes the reins." His smile was easy, and it was clear that this untouched plot held a special place in his heart. "It's my experiment," Bryce said, gesturing at the untamed beauty. "Letting nature take over, seeing what thrives."

I was fascinated despite myself. "It's a jungle."

Bryce chuckled. "More like a battleground. Every plant, every insect here is fighting for survival, for a place in the ecosystem. I don't come in here much, I just want to see what lives, and what nature can do for itself." He crouched down by a yellow plant and caressed a leaf. "And it's beautiful."

"Yeah, it is."

Only, I wasn't checking out the garden now. Instead, I was staring at Bryce, and losing myself in the softness in his expression, the peace, and the love in his words. My body did some weird things; my heart quickened, as if I was about to place a bet, as if…

And all the blood rushed south.

I wanted to taste his smile.

He stood and stepped back through the gate, gesturing for me to follow, and I was right up in his space. He touched my arm.

"It's okay," he said, but I wasn't sure what he was reassuring me for. I leaned toward him. I wanted to kiss him. I could lean in and taste all that love inside him and lose myself in all the things that made him happy.

And I swear, he leaned toward me, that damn expression so soft, and a flare of heat in his beautiful velvet-brown eyes.

"Daddy!"

Bryce jumped away, whirled, and caught an armful of young boy, sweeping him up into a wide hug. I knew he'd gone to pick up his son; he'd told me they'd seen the hockey game, he'd thanked me, but I'd never met the kid even though he'd been back a couple of days. Bryce said he was spending time with Aunt Katie and some cousins in the mornings, not that I'd listened. The kid was blond, blue-eyed, almost the opposite of Bryce, but he had his dad's chin, and yeah, his dad's smile.

"Dad, we did painting! It was so cool!" the kid announced, and then, noticed me. "Hi."

An older woman huffed and puffed her way up the path. "Sorry, Bryce, couldn't stop him!" she said with a grin, not at all worried it seemed.

"It's all good," Bryce said and hugged his son one last time before letting him down. "Leo, this is Michael who got us the tickets."

Leo stuck out a hand, and I could see flecks of green and orange on his fingers. I shook it solemnly, wondering if I should crouch, or was looming okay?

"Thank you for the tickets, Mr. Michael."

"You're welcome, and Michael is okay."

"Cool. So, I think I want to play hockey and be the one that does all the goal stuff. Can I ask you stuff?"

"I don't think Michael will want to be bothered," Bryce said in warning.

"I don't mind," I found myself saying.

What the hell?

Chapter 8

Bryce

"Are you serious with this?"

I nodded at Michael, wearing a smile that told him just how amusing this whole scenario was to me.

"It's a tradition here at the San Pedro Street Community Garden," I repeated for the fourth time as I held out a festive yellow Easter bonnet to the big, burly hockey player. "Everyone wears one for the Easter Egg Hunt."

I waved at the four other volunteers who had shown up on Holy Saturday to help with the tenth annual egg hunt. Every single one, including Leo, Mrs. Cho, and I, were decked out in secondhand bonnets from the nearby thrift shop. Mine was mint green with tiny—and rather moldy—fake sparrows glued to the brim.

"This is without a doubt the stupidest thing I have ever seen, and that includes witnessing you singing hippie songs to bees." He took the hat, slapped it down onto his head, then threw his hands outward in a "Happy?" motion.

"It looks cute," I teased, got a decidedly sour look, then bent down to pass along a tiny wicker basket filled with plastic eggs. Each egg had some candy in it, not that I was a big proponent of candy for kids—just ask Leo—but sliced veggies didn't hold up well inside plastic eggs. "So, what we do is we go and hide—"

"I know how egg hunts work. My parents used to do them all the time when Charles and I were little." Off he went with his pink basket and yellow Easter bonnet to stuff eggs under rhubarb plants. I took a moment to enjoy his backside, replaying that moment in the wild patch behind the gardens when we'd both leaned in to maybe kiss? I would have kissed him—no doubt in my mind—but should I have? Probably not. Yet, there was the urge to do so. To do more than kiss him if given half a chance. To spend a few languid hours exploring his body with my tongue as he writhed and—

"Dad, Mrs. Cho said that you need to get to the gate for the greetings!" Leo shouted as he barreled along one of the paths, his cheeks pink from exertion, one hand atop his head to hold his pale blue straw hat with tiny, flocked peeps in place. "I think there are at least two hundred people on the street! And they all have kids. So maybe like ten thousand people are here!"

I chuckled at his math, gave him a nod, and hurried

along in his wake to the front gates of the garden. There were perhaps fifty people here, with many children, all wearing outrageous bonnets as was tradition. I hadn't been lying. We even had a little hat contest after the egg hunt where one lucky person—not just lady—won a free basket of donated veggies for their holiday feast. And given that we were located in a rather poor section of town—Skid Row was not exactly affluent—and we had some drug-peddling issues, as well as far too many unsheltered souls, free food was a godsend.

Then, there was the recent rush of vandalism—a lemon tree branch here, a sign scratched there, the tag *S* and *O* was always at hand, and only yesterday, there'd been a small fire on a trestle laid out for planting that had left the ancient, scarred tabletop, even darker, and more gouged. I reported it to the local cops, but yeah, they weren't interested.

They already had their scapegoats in the homeless, but also reminded me that I had an ex-criminal working with me.

Whatever.

Ignore all of that. Focus on today.

I gave the gardeners on hand a quick peek. All were ready and smiling, even Michael, who stood by the shed looking silly and seductive all at once. Leo scurried up to my side. I grinned down at my son, gave his shoulder a squeeze, and unlocked the garden gate.

"Welcome! Welcome! Come on in! Line up around

the outside of the plots please. Oh, my goodness, Abigail, you look so lovely today! One of the scouts will take your bags. They are completely trustworthy. They're scouts after all." I directed the elderly woman who carried all her earthly belongings in a ratty carpetbagger's sort of tote to two young ladies in brown berets. The scouts rushed up to her, helped her to a seat in the shade, then brought her some pink lemonade from the office. We had a small table with cool drinks set up inside. Michael had moved to stand at the door of my office, arms folded, as if guarding the lemonade table. He still wore his bonnet. I found that endearing, which was bad on so many levels I couldn't count them if I used all my fingers and toes.

"Dad, stop staring at Michael and do the countdown!" Leo chirped as he gave my arm a quick tug.

"Right, the countdown," I said at the top of my lungs. "Are all you children ready to find the eggs that the Easter Bunny left?"

An eager shout of "Yes!" rose from the kids, so I counted from ten to one, then yelled at them to go. Off they went, Leo amid the poorest of the poor, giggling madly, as they rushed around like squirrels on Red Bull to find the most eggs. A few had to be reminded to be careful of the plants when one of Mr. Tyler's pea plants was snapped off accidentally. Thank goodness Mr. Tyler was a grandfather of four, so he was chill with a little plant damage if a child did it.

Thirty minutes passed, and once the mad rush slowed, parents fussed over the eggs in their children's baskets. Leo donated all his finds—without prompting from me—to some of the other searchers. I was proud of the kindhearted boy Courtney and I were raising. Then, we had the Easter Bonnet parade, where one person at a time would sashay to the opening in the middle of the garden, spin and show off their bonnet, then wait for the applause from the others in attendance.

Mr. Baciu, who owned the vacuum-repair shop two blocks west, won with the loudest cheers for his peacock-blue hat with white feathers. He was thrilled to take home a box of fresh veggies to the sickly mother and father he lived with.

Leo and I stood by the gate as our neighbors left, shaking hands, chatting, and wishing them all a joyous spring. When the gates were closed, I turned to find my volunteers tidying up the garden, Michael among them, his head still bedecked with his bonnet.

Leo ran over to him, leaving me to shuffle into my office to empty the dregs of the lemonade down my old, but beloved, double sink. As I was washing the punch bowl with some lemony dish soap, my son appeared at my side, his hat sitting on his head at a funny angle.

"Dad, can I play hockey?"

I rinsed the bowl and ladle, placed them on some paper towels on the drainer, and turned to my son.

"We'll have to discuss that with your mother when I take you home on Tuesday." I wasn't sure if he thought peppering me with that question at least three times per day would get him a different reply or not, but I was not saying yes before Courtney was brought up to speed. She and Tony had texted several times, sending images of themselves at various sites in Yellowstone. They looked so happy, all cuddly and lovey-dovey. I missed that. Not being cuddly with my ex-wife, but just being with someone whom I wanted to cuddle. Geysers at our backs optional.

"Michael says that the Storm has a youth team, and that it wouldn't cost gazillions of dollars if I signed up for that because… because all the hockey gear is donated by the players."

"That's good to know. We'll for sure mention that when we sit down with your mom."

His pout was legendary. Then, it vanished as his blue eyes rounded. "Oh, I told Michael to come to our place for Easter dinner tomorrow if he wanted to."

I gaped at my son. "Oh, well uhm…" I glanced through the open door to see Michael gathering up candy wrappers, dropping them into a small cloth sack he was carrying.

"Dad, you always say that no one should be alone on a holiday."

Was Michael going to be alone? Right. Yes, I'd said that numerous times. Why do kids recall off-handed mentions like that, but can't remember to pick up their dirty underwear?

"Sure, yes, that would be great. I'll tell him that—"

"Michael, Dad say's its cool for you to come to dinner with us!" Leo shouted out the door.

"Leo, for goodness sakes," I sighed, then trundled out to Michael. "We'd love to have you come over tomorrow."

"You don't have to do that, really. I know the kid asked me without clearing it with you first," Michael replied, then dropped a gum wrapper into his bag.

"No, it was remiss of me not to invite you. I just assumed that you'd be with your uhm, family?" His haunted gaze met mine, so I rushed ahead. "We're eating at four."

"Okay, thanks." He acted as if he wanted to say more, but Leo arrived, full of that kind of energy only seven-year olds possess and started talking hockey with Michael. Or perhaps I should say started talking hockey *at* Michael. I let them chat, slipping back into my office to work on quelling the rush of excitement making my tummy fizzy as ginger ale.

It meant nothing. The man was coming for dinner, it was not a date or anything of the sort. It was just a friendly meal offered in a caring manner to someone who was struggling. And Leo was right, no one should be alone on a holiday. Been there, done that, and it royally sucked.

I picked a bagful of cucumbers before leaving.

. . .

I<small>T WAS INSANE TO BE THIS JITTERY OVER A SIMPLE MEAL</small> for three guys.

I'd spent way too long in front of the mirror, tucking my pink shirt into my jeans, worrying if the white polka dots on it were too much, smoothing my navy tie, and trying to smooth my hair. I wasn't exactly letting my beard grow back, but my stubble was neat, and I'd tried so hard to look as if I hadn't spent an hour trying to get ready.

All he'd sent back after I'd texted him my address was a simple *OK*.

Okay to the address? Okay to coming?

And now, I was fretting over the fact the cucumber salad wasn't quite right. I'd added all the ingredients per Mrs. Cho's recipe. Honey, ginger, salt, rice vinegar, sesame oil, soy sauce, garlic, and chili paste.

"Leo, does this taste right?" I asked as I followed him around my small apartment with an oily cuke on a fork.

"Dad, stop. I ate fourteen cucumber slices already, and it's always gross," he whined, kicking off his slippers as the doorbell rang. "It's Michael!"

He thundered to the door, threw it open, then beamed up at the man in the doorway. I stood there in my *Hi Hungry, I'm Dad* apron, mouth tumbling open, cuke sliding off the fork to the carpet. Holy Jumping Jack Flash, the man cleaned up well. More than well.

He was stunning. Blue jeans, a silky green shirt, and darker green tie, his stubble perfection, and his short red hair combed and neat.

"Hey, I know I'm early..." Michael said as a form of greeting.

"You're in time for playing *Sonic Superstars!*" Leo grabbed his thick wrist.

"Leo, please, remember your manners. Michael, come in. Oh, thank you." He stepped into my very humble abode, stalled a few steps in, and handed me a bottle of sparkling grape juice.

"Non-alcoholic," he mumbled as he passed over the bottle.

"Thank you, this is very kind. We'll have some during dinner." I picked up the cuke resting on the carpet while Leo pulled Michael to the sofa. I hurried to the kitchenette, shoved the bottle into the fridge, and returned to meal prep. The vegan ham roast was close to done, the taters bubbling away, and the carrots were ready for a dousing of honey. And of course, the cucumber salad was... well, it was going to have to be what it was. I rushed about to set the table as Michael and Leo got into playing on the X-Box. They both shouted and hooted as the game progressed. Michael was close to being as animated as my son was, which was super cute.

I needed to get a handle on this attraction. It was not fitting at all, not given our situation. Still, every time I could sneak a peek, I was peeking. And I liked what I saw so much I nearly burnt the vegan ham.

After that close call, I focused on the meal, serving it, and then, watching as the guys dove in. Michael loved my cucumber salad. I could tell because he ate three servings. He did question the ham, which was understandable as the consistency was different than a real ham, but once I explained it was vegan, he muttered something about checking it out, then ate two slabs. We sipped bubbly grape juice throughout, and then, I made some coffee to go with the carrot cake I'd baked last night.

"Okay, this here is to die for," Michael said as he forked a large bite of cake into his mouth. I felt a blush tint my cheeks at his praise. "You really can cook."

"I enjoy cooking," I confessed, sitting back to give my tummy room. I'd wiggled into dress slacks for… well, I wasn't sure why to be honest.

Oh, come on Bryce, you know why, and he's sitting right across the table from you.

"Dad, can we watch *Hop* today?" Leo asked as he rubbed his belly. He'd done a fair job of eating his meal, even if he had skipped the gross cucumber salad.

"Sure, go cue it up. I'll be out as soon as I get the dishes washed." I stood as slowly as I could, giving the food in my gut time to slip down and not hit like a brick.

"I'll help," Michael announced, rising from his seat, then gathering dirty cake plates and coffee mugs.

"No, that's not necessary," I hurried to say, but he waved me off.

"Yeah, it is. You fed me, so let me help clean up," he stated as he carried the dishes to the sink. A walk of about four feet, if that. I shrugged in defeat. We worked side-by-side, him washing, his shirt sleeves rolled up exposing sexy forearms, and I dried, then put the dishes away. Leo was stretched out on the floor, his head on a throw pillow, sound asleep when we finally joined him to watch his movie.

Michael sat beside me, his elbows on his knees, wide shoulders straining the material of his shirt across his shoulders. I stopped looking. Eyes glued to the story of the son of the Easter Bunny who wanted to be a rock star, I did my best to tell myself this was just any other Easter afternoon. The aroma of Michael's aftershave was making it hard to pretend this was just any other holiday meal, though. As did the press of his knee against mine, or the way he darted looks my way as my son snored at our feet.

"I should go," he announced after our gazes met and held for so long it was getting awkward. He shot to his feet; I did the same, biting back the urge to ask him to stay.

"Of course. I'm sure you have other plans." I walked him to the door.

"Not really."

"Oh, well, you're more than welcome to hang out here."

It seemed the polite thing to say. He stared at me, his expression hard to read until he bent to kiss me. On the mouth. It took me aback for about one millionth of a second, and then, I was into the moment. He was taller than me by a few inches, so I had to tip my head a bit as he slid an arm around my middle. The softness of his lips, the taste of cream cheese icing on his tongue, and the firmness of his chest made me woozy. I clung to him tight, winding my fingers around his tie to ensure he, and his luscious mouth, went nowhere. I felt him shift, easing me against the door, his tongue tangling with mine. I let him move me where he wished, my body thrumming with lust. The kiss lingered, growing hotter as we grew harder, and then, Leo coughed. Just once. A sleepy sort of kid snuffle/cough. The kind he rarely woke up from, but that tiny sound was like someone dousing us with icy cold water.

Michael jerked away, my hold on his tie close to garroting him as he fumbled for the doorknob. "I… this was… I have to go."

I released his tie, nodding stupidly, my lips tingling as he barreled down the stairs leaving me in the doorway with an erection, puffy lips, and ten thousand self-recriminations.

Chapter 9

Michael

I SHOULDN'T HAVE DONE THAT.

I'd crossed a line.

My skin itched with want and need, my heart hurt, but my head screamed at me to step back and away because tangling all these inappropriate personal emotions with our professional relationship was wrong.

And Bryce, why hadn't he pushed me away? He must have felt it too, the wrongness of it. But he didn't stop it. Did he want this as much as I did? Or was it just a moment of weakness for him too?

I tapped the cab driver's seat. "Can you stop here, please."

He shot me a glance, then out at the empty road beyond. We were still two miles away from Charles's house, and all there was near here was parkland stretching for miles, with running routes and hill climbs. In addition to that, I knew he recognized me, although he didn't say anything, his frown and the LA Storm bobble head on his dash meant that he had to know me.

"Sure, buddy," he murmured and pulled over, and I thrust money at him, not caring what I gave him, then tumbled out of the car. "Hey, you okay? I mean, I know it's rough being professional and all that celebrity shit, and if you need me to take you somewhere, no questions asked…" He stopped before he added terms like rehab, which was what I'm sure he was thinking. Did I look as confused and worried as I felt?

"I'm all good," I said, putting up the barrier against all the bewilderment and pain, and letting confident-Michael out to play. "I'm early, so I'm walking." I flexed my arm and grinned. "Need to get the exercise in for when I get back."

He narrowed his eyes, almost as if he was going to call me on my shit, then he nodded. "Sure, sure."

I wish people would stop using that fucking word as if it meant something.

I gave a half wave as he left, but my smile dropped as soon as he vanished around the corner, and I was left on the side of the isolated trail. In seconds, I was into the trees, and I leaned against the first one that hid me from the road and bent at the waist, completely done.

I regretted kissing him.

But how could I regret a kiss so perfect?

How could I possibly ignore the magnetic pull, the undeniable attraction that had been building between us? Was it just me?

He'd kissed me back, right?

He'd wanted that part of me, even knowing why I was at the community garden, knowing some of my demons.

It had felt right in a way I couldn't put into words, but I was consumed with a gnawing regret, because I'd started to like Bryce—no, more than like—and that kiss was not only a crossing of a line. I was sure that Essie would sit in her therapy chair and stare at me with sympathy, and then, tell me I was taking a step down a familiar, dangerous path. Maybe even that I was replacing one addiction with another? I could hear her now, telling me the pattern was all too clear, a cycle of intense highs that I chased, regardless of the consequences.

My addiction consumed me.

It consumed me, and I lost everything.

I hurt people.

I let the team down. I let family down. They all hate me.

I deserve that.

The last thing I wanted was to cause any more harm, especially not to Bryce, not to the semblance of stability I had found in my work with him. But that kiss, as perfect as it was, had opened a door to something that freaking terrified me.

Deep breaths, and then, I headed along the trail and took the spur ending at Charles's side gate, pressing the numbers on the pad, and stepping inside, and to my horror, I realized that whatever Zhang family event he had going on, was still... *going on*.

And most of the team were hanging around the pool, the scent of food wafting my way, kids running in the yard, and so much laughter. I went back to the door, fumbled the handle—no one had seen me come in through the ornamental bushes—and I almost made it.

I saw Prez before he saw me. My heart pounded with something like fear that I hadn't felt since... well, before everything fell apart. Prez had been my best friend on the team, the one I relied on, but after the incident, he might as well have vanished.

He called my name, his voice slicing through the hum of the people, and I stiffened. I watched him jog over, that familiar look of easy camaraderie on his face that now seemed so foreign. I didn't want to do this— not here, not now.

"Hey, stranger," he said, his smile faltering as he read the room, the air between us thick with unsaid things. He cleared his throat. "How you doing?"

"With what?"

"Um..." He gestured around him, and I assumed he was talking about hockey.

"Apart from losing the only thing I was good at, fine." I knew I sounded bitter, and I waited for him to tell me that it was all on me anyway, that I deserved to lose my career, that this was why he'd kept his contact with me to infrequent messaging. "Anyway, I have things to do," I lied and turned to leave, to escape a confrontation I wasn't ready for.

"I'm sorry."

Those two words stopped me in my tracks.

Prez, my best friend from the team, the guy who knew when to fold his cards and walk away from the poker table, was now laying his cards out for me to see.

"Man, I should've seen it," Prez said, his voice low, tinged with a regret that seemed to hang heavy between us. "I should've kept pushing, should've stayed even when you didn't want me. I'm sorry I didn't try harder."

I could feel the tightness in my chest, the anger, and the hurt swirling together into a bitter cocktail. Prez had been there through it all, yet when things had gotten rough, when I started spiraling, he had stepped back like everyone else. Maybe, he thought he was giving me space, or perhaps, he didn't know what to do with the mess that was me. But hearing his apology now struck a chord because it wasn't all on him.

I SPUN AROUND, ANGER SURGING. "THIS ISN'T ALL ABOUT you, asshole." This wasn't about *his* guilt, *his* apologies, *his* reasons. "It was me. I was the one who said I didn't want to talk, I was the one who failed you, I pushed you away, and that is what addiction does—it destroys everything." Our friendship had failed when it faced its first real test, and it was all on me for shutting him out, the same as I'd shut Charles out, and anyone who wanted to help me. As I stood there, looking at the face of my once best friend, I wondered if there was anything left to salvage, or if some distances were just too great to bridge.

"I should have stopped you," Prez said, a little mournfully. "I could have forced you to…"

I stepped up into his space—I wasn't the tallest on the team, and Prez was a head higher, but I was a scrappy fucking hockey player, and he couldn't have done jack shit to force me to do anything. "Try and force me now," I challenged.

He stared at me.

And I stared back.

And then, somehow, everything cracked, and we were hugging, and it was more than a bro hug, it was something with meaning.

"Guys?" Charles's voice was like nails on a chalkboard, and I extricated myself from Prez's hug. "Okay?" he asked, his gaze flicking between us, concerned, confused.

I had this compulsion to reach out to him, to hug him…

To thank him…

But the kiss with Bryce, and the emotions, and the angst, and I was done.

"I have to go," I said, stepping back, and only just avoided Hope, who was roller-skating down the path.

"Red!" she exclaimed and did a fancy twirl, grabbing my leg to steady herself. "Up!" she demanded and held out her hands.

I couldn't do any more right now. I was panicking, my chest was tight, my head hurt.

"Later, Hope. Later."

And then, I ran, and locked the door of the pool house behind me.

This had been one fucked up day.

After a moment of concentrating on my breathing, I curled up on my sofa, my phone in my hand, and opened Google.

"Is it okay to kiss someone when…" I stopped and stared. I already knew all the answers about whether I should have fallen for the sexy gardener who clearly had his own issues. An unknown text *500* came up, and I deleted it, then the game score slid on my screen—the Rebels and Railers were tied at two each and heading for overtime.

"I bet the Railers will have that," I said to my empty room, then groaned. I didn't bet anything, even if Tennant Rowe in a shoot-out was a sure thing. I itched to re-download the betting app, and I had maybe a minute to do it. I scrolled to the store to get it. I found it. Then something stopped me.

Maybe it was honeybees, or Leo, or the stupid Easter hat thing, or it was talking to plants, seeing the wild garden, or maybe it was Prez admitting he felt guilt when he shouldn't at all. Maybe it was thinking that maybe Charles felt guilt as well when it was all on me.

Or maybe it was the kiss.

I closed the app.

Waited for the score as my skin itched with need.

Then, Tennant fluffed his shot, the puck hitting the metal, the clang of it deafening in my head.

That didn't mean the Railers had lost—it was all on Marquis, an unlikely shootout hero, and I waited with bated breath as he did his run, Bryan Delaney solid in the net.

But the lamp lit.

Marquis had scored, and the Railers had lost in OT.

How do I feel?

Should I feel good that I'd made it through this without betting on an outcome? Should I feel grateful I'd avoided losing again? All I felt was numbness.

I headed for Google again and typed in a long ass sentence.

"I'm addicted to gambling. I've lost everything, is it okay to feel nothing?"

I backspaced because that wasn't the question I wanted to ask. "I'm addicted to gambling. I've lost everything, is it okay to kiss someone?"

There was only one answer—a link to a national

helpline, and I clicked on the link, which was nothing that I didn't already know.

I *am* an addict.

I *am* addicted to gambling.

I feel a high the same as a drug addict. I feel the numbness of an alcoholic. I feel the low…

I feel…

Something tickled my face, and I wiped at it, and my hand came away wet.

What?

I MANAGED TO AVOID BRYCE FOR EXACTLY TEN MINUTES. I know that because I arrived at five-fifty a.m. to hide in the shed with the mowers, and at six, there he was, right up in my space, looking uncomfortable and weirded out. I picked up a plastic flower pot as if that was what I'd come in to find.

Hell, I could understand his unease—after all, I bet it wasn't every day the people he was watching over threw themselves into a kiss, then pushed against him and… yeah.

"We need to talk," Bryce said. No ifs, no buts, it was straight into it.

"Okay." I put the pot down.

"We understand each other's struggles intimately, and I know it's not immediately obvious what the drawbacks of diving into a relationship can be, when we're both addicts, but the lines between support and co-dependency blur too easily." he began, as if he were reading from a self-help manual. "You'd think that we could be each other's support, but every time one of us feels the pull of old habits, it wouldn't just be a personal battle, it would be a shared risk. If I think I can't handle things…" He sighed. "The fear of relapse doubles, and along with that there is all the pressure to—"

"It was just a kiss," I blurted, stopping him in his tracks.

He blinked at me in the shadowy space, then nodded. "Sure," he offered.

"What does that even mean! Sure. Do you agree with me that 'sure it was just a kiss,' or 'sure,' you agree, or you disagree, or you're in the middle, or—"

He cut me off with a finger to my lips, and we stood in silence for a moment.

"Sure, I know you *think* it was just a kiss," Bryce began. "But actually, for me, it was more than just a kiss, it was seeing glimpses of the parts hidden behind *superstar hockey player*, or *addict*, and being fucking scared about what you could mean to me if I let you." He scrubbed at his eyes, and he looked tormented.

"Oh." The meaning of his words terrified me and stole any rational response I could think up.

He stepped closer, cradled my face, and I wanted to freaking cry.

For fuck's sake.

Then, he kissed my forehead with a soft brush of his lips, and it was nothing like the wildness of what we'd done at his house.

It was heartbreaking, simple and gentle.

And then, he left.

"It scares me too," I whispered to the empty shed.

I'm so fucking scared of everything.

Chapter 10

Bryce

All too soon Easter break was over.

It just about killed me to pack up Leo's clothes and herd him out of the door at the crack of dawn. Despite his mother urging us to fly, I insisted on driving. This way, I could drag out the time with my son a little longer. He was bleary-eyed when we left, napping most of the morning until we arrived at Hoover Dam. We both enjoyed the tour and a fast bite, which we had in a countrified chain restaurant near the power station.

We pulled into the driveway of Courtney's quaint little house about four in the afternoon. She came rushing out of the house in shorts, a tee, and bare feet to gather her child into her arms. They hugged for a long time, my smile fading when I spied Tony in the doorway. Ugh. That man was just too everything.

Leo broke free from his mother to jog to Tony and embrace him.

"Hey," Courtney said, stepping into my line of sight, Leo's bag over her shoulder, "you look like you're watching a hawk eating your favorite chicken." I smoothed out the lines etched into my brow. "Much better. Why don't you come in and have dinner? It's just pepperoni pizza and ice cream, but it will fill you up for the drive home. Or you could crash on our sofa and leave tomorrow?"

That offer yanked my attention from the man trying to horn in on being Leo's dad to my ex-wife.

"Why are you being so nice?" I asked, got a look, and amended my previous statement. "Not that you're not always nice, but dinner and a bed? What's wrong?"

"Nothing is wrong. I'm just trying to open channels of communication between you and Tony. Leo should see you two getting along and not eying each other warily."

Okay, sure, she made a good point but… ugh, Tony. "Sure, yes, of course. Pizza sounds good. I'll skip sleeping on the sofa, though. I need to get back to LA."

"I'm sure the garden can tend itself. Mrs. Cho and your volunteers can pick potato bugs off the chili peppers in your stead."

"Courtney, potato bugs are found on potatoes, hence the name potato bug," I teased and got a playful swat on the arm. She was never into gardening as I was, not even before the pills rocked our world, and especially not after. "I'll get a hotel if it runs too late."

She let it drop, turning to enter her home. I trudged

along in her wake, wishing I'd said no to her offer. Tony met me inside the door with a warm smile and a handshake. Why? Why was this guy so damned nice? And hot? And in total control of his life. He'd never taken a tumble off a stage in a smoky nightclub. Never fallen under the spell of painkillers. Never driven his wife and baby son out of the state. Never been in rehab or gone to a group or hidden away in a city garden to shelter from the storm that was life outside the garden walls. Nope. Not Tony Micheletti. Ugh. Just… ugh.

"You're looking well," Tony informed me, pumping my hand, his sparkling smile blinding me. "We sure did miss Leo, but it sounds as if you two had a great time."

"Yes, my *son* and I always have wonderful visits," I replied, releasing his hand. He nodded, and it was clear he was getting the point because his smile dipped a little. Shit, I was a petty man at times.

"Why don't we get to the pizza before it's cold?" He gave me a bro-slap on the shoulder.

I led the way because I did know the layout of my son's house in case he thought otherwise. The kitchen was small, but cheery, the fridge covered with Leo's artwork, school calendars, and appointment cards for dentists and doctors. Courtney was doling out pizza, Leo was sitting in his chair sipping root beer from a bottle, and Tony slipped up beside Court to peck her cheek. She beamed and giggled before handing him a plate of pizza, then hip-checking him gently away from her side. "Bryce, are you still avoiding meat?"

"I am," I answered, taking a seat on the end of the table that was rarely used. The chair had some light dust on the rungs. That made me feel even odder to be here with them. Like a third wheel or some creepy specter. "Thank you."

She smiled as she placed two thick slices of pizza minus the pepperoni in front of me. Tony cracked open a bottle of root beer, handed it over, then grinned at my ex as she sat down with one slice holding double the pepperoni.

"Well, this is nice," she said, her gaze touching on Leo, then Tony, and at last, me. "I'm glad we could do this. We never eat a meal together."

I grunted something in reply, unsure of mentioning that sitting here and making small talk with Tony was akin to running into a hornet's nest on purpose over and over.

"Jack sends his regards," she murmured.

I side-eyed her. "Your brother sends his regards to your ex?" I half whispered.

She took a small bite of her pizza, placed it back in her paper plate, then wiped her hands on the napkin lying on her lap. "Well, not so much his regards, but a hello, I guess."

"Yeah right."

"So, while we have everyone here, Tony and I would like to make a small announcement." Courtney was anxious now.

I lowered my slice to my plate as a subtle warning

bell sounded in my head. The kind I'd learned to heed from my days in rehab. The soft peal of a klaxon warning of an incoming upheaval.

My gaze flew to her left hand. There it sat. A small diamond engagement ring. I wouldn't even noticed. How had I not? Lord above, I was oblivious. I tried to work up some spit but couldn't. Tony took her right hand and gave it a squeeze. Leo was chewing pizza, cheeks filled to bursting, staring at his mom.

"Right, well, Leo, your mom said yes to my proposal," Tony explained to my son. I sat there, stunned, unable to even begin to consider what this would mean to our little family dynamic. Not that this family was mine, not really, but in a way it was. Well, half of it was. Leo was mine. I stopped watching Tony to instead focus on Leo. He was confused but working on a smile since all the adults—well two adults, as one was sitting there like a stoned moose—were smiling at him. "Your mom and I are going to get married," Tony added, then we waited, with baited pizza breath, to see how the child would respond.

Leo stared right at me. "Are you still going to be my dad?"

It felt as if my whole world cracked open in that instant. I got up, knelt beside my son, and took his face between my hands.

"I will *always* be your dad, always. No one will *ever* replace me, not ever." I tossed a glance at Tony who, kudos to him, nodded. Courtney was teary already.

When I glanced back at my son, he seemed less bewildered. "I'm your dad forever, and perhaps someday, if he's super cool like me, Tony might be your stepdad, but he has to earn that right."

"And I will, buddy," Tony interjected as Courtney sniffled into a paper napkin with yellow flowers printed on it. "I'll work so hard to be the best stepdad in the world. And I promise to make your mom as happy as a man can."

"Okay," Leo whispered. I pressed a kiss to his forehead, gave him a shaky smile, and returned to my seat. My boy turned to his mom. "Are you going to give me a baby brother or sister after you're married?"

Courtney choke/laughed. Tony's dark eyes widened, but then, he chuckled as well. I plastered on the happiest face that I could, nibbling at my pizza as the happy couple, and my son, starting discussing wedding plans. After the meal was done, Leo gave me a hug, then walked me to my car, a sneaky exit from the whole wedding prep chatter. Courtney and Tony stood in the door, her tight to his side, waving as I said goodbye to Leo.

I was not staying over, nor was I getting a hotel. I needed some distance. Not from my son, but from the man who'd vowed not to usurp me, but who might anyway.

"Are you cool with Mom and Tony's announcement?" I asked, one knee on the warm driveway, one leg bent, Leo in front of me. He nodded.

"If you're feeling funny about it, or anything, you know you can talk to your mom, right?" He bobbed his head. "Or your Uncle Jack." It killed me to mention Uncle Jack—I wanted Leo to always come to me, but as much as Jack hated me, he wasn't a bad guy, and he was a good uncle.

"Yeah."

"But you have my number. You can call me anytime to talk. About anything. Your mom looks really happy, don't you think?"

"I guess." He heaved a mighty sigh. "Why can't you marry her again?"

Oh boy.

I reached up to smooth down his wild hair. Did little boys ever have combed hair? I had yet to see it.

"Well, we're both in different places in our lives. Mommy is happy with Tony now."

"Are you happy with Michael?"

My mind blanked. "I… what do you mean?"

"I saw you two kissing on Easter," he stated calmly.

"Ah well, that was… it's complicated, Leo."

"Grown-ups *always* say that" he huffed, and it was clear he was put out. A small bat flew overhead. It was past time for me to go. I had an eight hour drive to make yet.

"Well, sometimes life, and people, are just complicated, buddy. But as for me and your mom, that part of our lives is over. She's with Tony now, and she is super happy. That's good, right?"

"Yeah, I guess." He toed a rock in the driveway with the tip of his Spiderman sneaker. "Will you marry Michael?"

This child, oh my stars. "I'm not sure what will happen with Michael... hey, look up at me." I tipped his chin a bit. His gaze met mine. "Relationships are tricky, but if I ever do find another person to love and decide to marry them, I will discuss it with you first, okay?"

"Okay. I like Michael. He's nice, even though he pretends to be grumpy."

"Yeah, he is," I agreed, kissed his head, and sent him back to his mother and his... Tony waiting at the door.

I DROVE UNTIL MIDNIGHT, PULLED INTO A DINER JUST OFF of I-8, and sat there for the longest time, sipping coffee, and pushing a double chocolate donut around a blue-and-white checkered plate. My head was packed with a dozen warring emotions. I needed some time and space to process everything.

Lost in thoughts ranging from sadness to jealousy to confusion, I ran my finger over the map on the coffee-stained placemat. Yes, I was sad. Should I be? Probably not, but there it was. Although, they told us in group that no emotion was wrong, so sure, be sad Bryce. Be mad, be happy, be scared, be ashamed, be gloomy. They were all valid feelings. The life I'd been living was now in disarray. My ex was getting married, my son would have a new father, and the man who worked under me was tempting me in ways I hadn't been tempted since my dark days.

It felt like too much all at once. My finger moved over the state of Arizona, crossing the border into California where a picture of the state bird sat in the middle of the Sonoran Desert. I tapped the drawing of the California quail. The desert always called to me in times of upset. I'd done my rehab in a small facility in Barstow, and part of my recovery, I always claimed, was due to the desert songs. Songs sung by the Scott's orioles as they flitted among the Joshua trees. Songs I'd penned, stuffed into a folder, and had never played or sung. Maybe someday, I would dig them out…

So, knowing what I needed to do to center myself, I placed a midnight call to my supervisor, waking her from a deep sleep, and told her I was taking the two weeks of vacation that I had accrued over the past five years. She informed me that I had way more than two weeks, then asked if everything was okay. I assured her that it was. So, with my garden covered for the next fourteen days, I booked a motel that cost about fifty bucks a night, got back into my car, and drove to the Happy Gila Hotel located a mere five miles from Joshua Tree National Park.

The room was dingy, but clean enough for me. I settled in, sent a text to Mrs. Cho to let her know I was taking a sabbatical in the desert and to keep an eye on the volunteers. She was still asleep but would reply when she woke up. I debated over texting Michael, but that seemed like a step too far since we were… well, what we were was part of the reason I was here watching the sunrise over the desert through a smudged motel window. Maybe a couple of weeks apart would be good for both of us. Perhaps, we would find the resolve to keep our hands—and our lips—to ourselves.

Chapter 11

Michael

It had been a week since I'd last seen Bryce. Instead, it was Clem, someone Bryce had put in charge, and someone I didn't know so well, who was signing off on my hours. Our interactions were very different from my times with Bryce.

"Got your hours logged," Clem said, staring at the clipboard.

"Thanks," I replied, missing Bryce's talks about bees and plants and anything else he could throw at me before I left for the day.

Clem nodded, all business, no chit-chat about nature or life. The connection I had felt with Bryce, that ease of conversation, was absent. I realized how much I'd come to appreciate Bryce's presence, his way of making even community service feel a bit less like a chore.

In the days that followed, I found myself missing

Bryce more than I expected. The way he talked about nature, his enthusiasm for the garden, it was infectious. It wasn't only his knowledge about bees or plants, it was the way he made everything seem interesting, the way he listened and made me feel heard. His absence was more than a simple change in routine; it was a missing piece in my day-to-day recovery, a reminder of the connection we had started to build.

I remember asking Mrs. Cho where Bryce was, and her reply was so nonchalant it took me by surprise. "Oh, he's off meditating," she said, as if that explained everything.

To her, Bryce seeking solitude for meditation was normal, but to me, it sounded like something from another world, far removed from the chaos of my own life. The idea of Bryce finding peace in such a quiet, introspective way added to the layers of him I was only now beginning to understand. Almost as if he was closer to nature than he let on.

Lost in thought, I was staring at a sunflower, marveling at its intricate patterns, when my phone's ringtone jolted me back to reality. The sharp sound broke the garden's tranquil silence, a harsh reminder of the world beyond this peaceful sanctuary, and I scrambled to stop it.

A call from Coach Hudain? That couldn't be right.

"We're looking at next season, Michael," the coach's voice came through the line before I could even say hello. "Wanted to get your thoughts."

I paused, a mix of emotions swirling inside. "On the Storm?"

"Jesus. Why else would I be calling?" He was tense.

I replayed what I'd asked, and I guess it was a stupid thing to say, but still… anyway, I wasn't sure why he'd be calling with anything to do with the Storm at all. He'd been one of the most vocal in wanting me gone, pointing out that I'd fractured the team, about how tired he was of my shit, late to practice, not giving even fifty percent in games, that I was only there because my brother was captain and covered my ass.

"I haven't thought much about the team. I've been… dealing with other things." I didn't know why I was hedging—he knew what I'd been going through, and what I was dealing with.

There was a brief silence. "Sounds about right." Was that sarcasm? It sure sounded like mockery, with a hint of derision and some added exasperation.

"I love the team, you know that. I didn't mean for all of this to blow up, I never put them together—"

"Well, we know that, *Zeetoo*."

Michael, my name is Michael. I shoved back my own irritation because I *had* let the team down, and I did owe Coach something, however much he hated me.

"Um, if you want me to take a look at the lineup, or some of the rookies, and give some pointers. I mean, I saw you traded for that New York D-man, Oliver Cowan? He's a good guy, but slowing down now, and our forwards are too fast for him, maybe? So, he'd need to work with Charles and fix that." Hope was butterflies in my chest. Maybe, I hadn't fucked up everything as bad as I thought. Hell, it would be strange, being on the outside looking in, but it was a start, and maybe a small reconnection to the world I once lived and breathed.

"Jeez, Michael, this is nothing to do with what you bring on the ice," Coach said tiredly. "I didn't even want to call, but apparently your jersey sales, the fans, the team's image... there's a lot of pressure from management to figure out what you're worth to the team."

I felt a pang of disappointment.

No, it wasn't just a pang—I was destroyed.

This call didn't come from a place where a man I admired had a genuine belief in me, but rather, he'd been forced to call me by people more interested in the dollar signs I represented. "I understand," I replied, trying to mask my disappointment.

What had I expected? A fatted calf and a hero's welcome?

"Yeah well, I'm not happy about it either, but Jesus, if I have to have you back at some point, then for fuck's sake keep up the conditioning, get on the ice, stay sharp, and if they say I have to, then... yeah... bye."

The call ended so abruptly I stared at my phone for a while, wondering if I'd imagined it. I hadn't even considered the complexities of a potential return to hockey, and it hurt to be reduced to a profit line item, more than about the hockey itself.

I was keeping up my fitness, working in the garden improved muscle groups I didn't even know I had, but actual skating hadn't happened in months.

I tried to refocus on the sunflower, attempting to count its petals in an effort to regain my calm, stretching each aching muscle, but the sound of shouting in the distance was a persistent noise, pulling my attention away. We didn't often have shouting around here—the last time was me shouting at Bryce about manure, and then the two of us cracking up because manure was funny.

I missed Bryce.

Only the shouting sounded as if someone was scared, and I realized it was coming from the direction of Bryce's office and the sheds beyond. With reluctance, I left the sunflower behind, heading towards the source of the commotion, ready to find out what was happening, and catching the scent of smoke way before I got there.

There wasn't supposed to be fire here—Bryce had given me a long rambling speech about fire danger in LA, and how even though traditionally fire led to life, or something, bonfires were banned here.

So, what was the smoke?

"Someone help!"

My jog turned into a sprint, and I leaped at least two small hedges, apologizing to the gardener whose lettuces I'd squashed, and skidded to halt by the sheds. There was a fire, a wooden shed, and Mrs. Cho holding a bucket. She was throwing water, but that wasn't going to help, we needed a hose. I helped a couple of kids from a neighboring plot drag the hose over, and settled them in to water down the flames, noticing that Mrs. Cho was getting way too close. I jumped the hose, and the discarded bucket, and grabbed the small woman around the waist before rolling us away from the shed, and just in time as the structure creaked and groaned. The fire was out, the wood smoldering, and with a bang the whole structure collapsed in on itself, splinters flying.

I don't know what was in there, but we'd have to dig everything out.

Mrs. Cho eased herself out of my hold muttering something about idiots. I'm sure she didn't mean me, after all, I'd saved her from getting squashed by a collapsing shed.

Right?

I MADE IT TO THE END OF THE DAY, DIRTY FROM WORKING on pulling the shed apart. There were candles inside, nothing insidious, no one had meant for the fire to happen, but it was hard work trying to ease apart the scorched wood and melted appliances stored inside, including a small lawnmower, and several hoes and forks. Between me and a couple of other guys, we'd managed to save what we could, then carted off what we couldn't, and now, all I wanted was a shower and bed.

Charles was picking me up, and he and Hope grinned at me as I approached, only his grin dropped when I got closer.

"What the f—fudge happened to you?" he asked, bewildered, glancing at his leather interior.

"Small fire in a shed," I said, then slid into the front seat, offering Hope a small high-five, which she met with ease, then screwed up her nose at the smell.

"You're okay?" Charles asked, as if he were worried.

"Of course I am." I shut the concern down, belted up, and indicated he should drive.

"Asshole," he muttered under his breath, the sounds of a Disney movie in the back seat drowning everything else out. "Can't even be worried about my own fudging brother."

I ignored him, stared out of the window, and didn't have an ounce of jealousy over his beautiful SUV that wasn't even the best of the cars he owned.

Nope.

No jealousy at all, just a ton of self-pitying, missing-Bryce, dirt, and funkiness.

Chapter 12

Bryce

I'D BEEN HOME FOR THREE HOURS WHEN A SOLID *THUMP* on the door yanked me from the scribblings I was making on a sheet of paper. Stirring about, stretching my legs, I shook off the creative mindset as my stiff back popped. I'd been lost in songwriting since I'd stepped into my stuffy place. The desert always inspired me, not only creatively, but spiritually. I could find myself on the dunes. Glancing about at the sheets of paper scattered around me, I had to snicker. My guitar rested on my lap, the last chords fading into the late afternoon sun peeking through the window.

Another *thump*, this one stronger, brought my attention back from that hazy, out-of-body place I visited when I was making music. Much like artists and writers fell into a zone where the work consumed them.

"Come in," I shouted, certain it was Mrs. Cho coming up to check on me, then press me for information on why I hadn't come back when I'd said I would. She was the mother I wished I had. The door creaked open. I craned my head to glance back at my landlady to see Michael standing there, staring in at me with mild trepidation. "Oh," I commented, placing my six-string aside. "I thought you'd be Mrs. Cho coming to pump me full of soup."

"No, it's me, and I don't have any soup."

"Well, come in," I said, shifting off my tender backside. Sitting on the floor wasn't as pleasant a pastime as it used to be. Still, it was where I went when the muse found me. I watched him close the door, toe off his sneakers, then make his way to the chaos area. "Here, sit." I shuffled some papers and folders out of the way next to me.

He lowered himself down, long strong legs in cargo shorts folding into a loose lotus. "I was scared I'd find you lying in here dead or something. Mrs. Cho said you went to the desert because you were having a crisis."

I rolled my eyes. "No, nothing that severe. I was just… in a place of confusion."

"Ah, like that old Genesis song," he said as he lifted a sheaf of paper filled with words and chords. He stared at the music, then glanced back to me. "This is pretty deep stuff, Bryce."

"It was a pretty deep time on the dunes," I said, hoping like hell he'd not read the lyrics to the song I had just penned about him. The floor was littered with tunes, many jotted down on bar napkins or placemats from rusty spoons. I'd never spent a more productive time among nature than the past two weeks. I smiled, leaning to the left to peek at the paper in his hand. "That's an older song. I wrote that when I was in rehab. Pretty dark."

"Yeah, no shit." He stared hard at me, searching for something. "What did you do to get this dark and deep?"

"You don't want to hear that story now," I said, then sighed, moving around to face him, easing closer to breathe in the crisp smell of his cologne.

"But you'll tell me someday?"

I leveled a stare at him. "You haven't earned the right to see my dark side," I said, and he winced, then gave me sad puppy dog eyes. I had to change the subject. "I heard you were a fire hero."

"Whatever."

"Mrs. Cho was talking you up."

"She called me stupid."

I laughed at that. "She calls everyone stupid." I strummed some more. "Cops said it was an accident," I added. "Typical. It's not like they're taking notice of anything that happens, say we're insured and that's it. Any sign of vandalism, and they blame the people outside the gate, or the gardeners themselves."

"Yeah," Michael murmured, although I don't think he was listening. I knocked his elbow.

"I want to tell you what I came to realize on my sabbatical."

"What?"

"That flirting with you is a bad thing."

"It is?"

"Yep. You're an addict, I'm an addict, and as much as I think about kissing you, I know that—"

"Wait, you spend time thinking about kissing me?"

I placed my guitar next to me. "Don't act like you don't know," I cautioned him.

"Whatever."

We stared at each other, so close, and all the good intentions I'd come to hold close went flying out of the window when his tongue darted out to wet his lips. Uh oh.

Then, he lunged at me, and down we went, his mouth on mine. Papers and pens crinkled and shifted under me. I grabbed at whatever part of him I could find. Arms, shoulders, hips. He grunted as our tongues met, pressing into me with a slow bump-and-grind any stripper would envy. He had quick, powerful hands, and before I could pull in a breath to tell him to go faster, he had our flies open and our cocks out.

"Ah," I did gasp as he took us both in hand, his rough fingers squeezing so perfectly I almost came apart. "You haunted me," I confessed, my lips next to his ear. He growled low and deep, placing a mark on my exposed shoulder that sent hot white sparks to my groin. "Followed me through the sands, your eyes among the stars when I viewed them at midnight."

"I missed you," he whispered, nipped at my throat, and then, pumped harder, his orgasm hitting him. I cried out, following him over the precipice, shudders racking me so hard I feared I might black out. Then, he kissed me, swallowing my whimpers of pleasure, his cock kicking, his cum mixing with mine. The slip and slide was exquisite.

We lay there next to my guitar, amid the various slips of paper and napkins, panting, eyes now locked.

"What next?" I enquired, my cock still resting beside his in his strong grip.

"I don't have a fucking clue," he replied, stealing a soft kiss, then tucking himself away before pushing to his feet to stagger to my front door, hand on the wall for support. I sat up, skin still tingling from my release, shoved my dick into my pants, then zipped and smiled at his wide back as he stalled. Head down, gripping the frame, breathing like a bull that had just run through the streets of Pamplona. "I should go. Tell me to go, Bryce."

I should have told him to go, but I didn't want him to leave.

"I'd rather you stay," I replied. He turned to face me; his expression impossible to read. "If you want. We could talk. I think that's something we really need to do."

"What if I'm tired of talking?"

"Then we don't talk." He shrugged. "So, are you staying?"

Chapter 13

Michael

"I CAN'T," I SAID, WITH GREAT REGRET. "YOU KNOW THAT I can't."

"I know," he murmured.

I appreciated his understanding, but I knew I had to tread with caution. The path to recovery was fragile, and while being with Bryce was everything I wanted in this moment, I couldn't risk veering off course. There was an undeniable attraction, his calm demeanor, like this soft light that grounded me, and his gentle tone had been casual, but inviting.

I didn't want casual. This wasn't only sex, and I was aware of where it might lead. The possibility of more intimacy with Bryce was tempting, but I was just beginning to find some balance.

"Bryce, I… it's not that I don't want to," I started, trying to articulate the storm inside me. "I've been to seven Gamblers Anonymous meetings, and I'm not sure my higher power is God or anything, but I know I have to change, and it has to come from within me, and being with you might…" I swallowed hard. "You might become my new addiction," I confessed, watching him.

He took a moment, then nodded with gravity. "I get that. How has GA been for you?"

"It's… different," I said, searching for the right words. "I'm not sure if I buy into everything they say, but it's making me think. About choices. About responsibility. I mean, it's definitely a shift," I continued, feeling the weight of my own words. "I listen to these stories, see these people who've lost so much, and it's like holding up a mirror."

"It's hard," Bryce agreed.

"It's like…" I deflated and slumped to the chair near the door. I should go, but I'd had all this realization and epiphany shit, and I wanted him to know at least some of my thought process, so it all tumbled out of me. "I have this self-destructive streak, right?" I stopped and thought about how to put it in language that made sense to me. "See, I'm like the goalie who leaves the net open."

"I thought you played on the wing?" Bryce said, confused. "Not that I know too much about hockey."

"It's an analogy. Go with it." He nodded, still confused. "So, if I was a goalie, then I'd have one job in the team, right? Guarding the goal, would be my life." Nope, I wasn't sure I was making sense, but I carried on anyway. "But there I go, chasing after the puck in the corners of high stakes and fast living, leaving my post unattended. Every time I gamble to throw myself into the next adrenaline rush, it's like I'm letting in goal after goal, betraying the team I'm supposed to be a part of. I'm playing every position except my own, and my life, my team, pays the price." My shoulders ached with tension, and I tried to relax as Bryce's expression softened.

"I understand," he murmured, and I knew he did, even with my half-assed hockey analogies.

"Starting a relationship now just doesn't seem right. I'm skating on thin ice, struggling to stay upright in my own life. How can I invite someone else into this fight against my addiction? It's like being in the middle of a game, down by goals, and already I'm not just playing for myself, but for someone else's heart too. It's not just my recovery on the line then; it's your well-being, your peace of mind. I've got to get my own play sorted before I team up with someone else."

Silence, and then, he smiled in that understanding, all-knowing way of his.

"I'm proud of you."

The words hit me; my chest tightened, and I rubbed at it with the heel of my hand. I saw his gaze drop there, and when he tensed, I knew I didn't have to explain why I was leaving. He knew that I could slip so easily, and that I needed that buzz of someone being proud of me and that was where this thing with Bryce could go horribly wrong. Him being proud of me as a mentor, as someone who clocked me in and out of my community service, was a million steps away from the basis for a real relationship. Somehow, in understanding that, I felt a mixture of relief and resolve. Maybe, at last, this was me on the right path.

"You've got to do what's right for you…" He pointed at his chest. "Whatever I feel in here, it's not the right time for us."

"What do you feel?" Shit. Why did I ask that?

"Other than you are so hot it burns, and I want you more than anyone I've ever been with?"

"Bryce," I near whined.

He threw me a rueful smile. "I feel possibility."

His words were so damn understanding, yet they left me more conflicted. I was at the beginning of navigating my way through my addiction, just starting to understand my own strength and the power to change. Taking this step, as appealing as it was, felt like it could unravel the fragile progress I'd made. I had to stay focused, even if it meant walking away from what Bryce offered.

"I feel that too," I admitted. "You're a good man, Bryce, and I see all the possibilities, but…"

"You need to go," he finished for me.

"Yeah. I have some amends to make, people to talk to. I need to work my way through this sentence, and come out the other side a better man, and then, I'll come find you."

"I'll see you tomorrow," he said.

I went to the door, opened it, the late night spilling into the room, a gusty breeze, and the scent of gardens. "I'll be here."

"Hey."

Charles whirled to face me, almost face planting into the pool, the long net he was using to clean it was the single thing that stopped him from falling in. I'd never understood why he didn't get a pool guy to do it, after all, Charles was paid more than I ever was, and yet, he'd always said the work kept him honest.

I hadn't understood that before.

"What the fuck!" he exclaimed, then glanced around him guiltily, probably checking for his daughters. We were alone, which was why now was the best time to talk to him, when I could be open and honest, and ask him to do me a favor that he could just as easily throw back in my face.

"My bad," I said with an attempt at a smile.

"What's wrong?" he asked with immediate concern, laying down the net, before stepping into my space, a hand on my arm. "Michael?"

"I'm heading out to a meeting," I began.

"Cool." It was obvious he had no idea what to say to me, and I'd done that—destroyed whatever we might have had with my insecurities and my gambling. "It sounds like there's a but coming," he said, and frowned.

"Well, yeah, but no, I mean, there's no but, I called a cab."

"Do you uhm… need money?"

The fact that he controlled my account was yet another wall between us, and he couldn't quite meet my gaze.

"No."

He glanced around, as if he was expecting something to jump out at him. In fact, the only time I'd ever seen my big brother on edge like this was the year of my draft. He'd been so desperate for me to end up with the Storm, wanted to do amazing things together —his words, not mine—and when it seemed as if the Raptors might take me, he'd had this same expression.

Heartbreak.

Sadness.

Expecting the worst.

"Will you come with me?" I blurted, and he blinked, his mouth dropping open. "It's one month, and I get a chip, and they said I could bring family, and you could see what—oomph."

He yanked me into a hug, then stood me away from him. "Cancel the cab. I'll drive. Give me five. "

He disappeared into the house to grab a jacket and change out of his shorts with the Storm logo, and came back dressed smartly, and it looked as if he'd done his hair. I remembered days when I used to stand next to him, younger than him, trying to tame my red hair into the same waves he had, wondering if I should dye it black like his. Then, maybe, I'd fit in with my dark-haired adoptive parents and brother. I never gave up despite how straight my copper-red hair was. Clare was at the back door, and she waved at me before throwing me a cautious smile.

I waved back—just as cautious—but I wasn't ready to go over and discuss what was happening. Charles and I needed to get on with it before I lost the need to open up this part of my life to the brother I'd always idolized and failed to live up to.

We didn't talk in the car, as Charles wound his way through the LA traffic, and ended up at the community hall, parking at the end of the row, then smoothing his jacket.

"Do I look all right?" he asked.

I glanced down at my worn jeans and the Storm sweater. "Better than I do," I deadpanned.

He frowned again and seemed regretful. "I'm sorry, I didn't mean to. I can take off the…"

I stopped his hand. "It's all good."

"I don't want to look as if I…" He stopped, and embarrassment flooded his face.

"As if you've got it together when the rest of us in there haven't?" I deadpanned. "Just, for god's sake, don't mention lottery tickets, and you'll be fine."

He paled. "Lottery tickets? Shit. Is that a trigger? Should I be aware of what I say? Maybe I won't say anything. Although, I'm not sure I've ever talked about lottery tickets in my life. Fuck."

We stared at each other, and then, I rolled my eyes. "I was yanking your chain."

He immediately deflated. "You're an ass, Mikey," he said without heat.

I held out a fist, and he bumped it. "Let's do this."

The Gamblers Anonymous meeting was the same as always, a circle of chairs and a pot of coffee. I fidgeted in my seat, Charles next to me, waiting for my turn to speak, and that was when Kevin introduced himself. Charles didn't know this, but he'd become my sponsor a week ago, a baseball fanatic who'd made a jab at hockey within the first two minutes of our first conversation. He was tall and slim, his gray hair and the lines on his face mapping out a long journey with gambling and an alcohol addiction, who was now in his seventeenth year of recovery. When I'd listened to his story of strength, it was humbling, and when he offered to be my sponsor, I couldn't help but feel a glimmer of hope.

When they called my name for the one-month chip, I felt every eye in the room on me. Walking to the front, I felt the familiar rush of being in the spotlight surge through me, but tonight, I didn't want it. I took the chip, my heart hammering, not from the attention, but from what it represented.

"Thanks," I managed to say, my voice a mere whisper, the usual grandstanding stripped away to reveal me, just Michael, the guy trying to get better.

I hurried back to my seat beside Charles, grateful

for the shelter of his silent support, catching Kevin's eye and exchanging nods. The applause was warm, but all I could think was, let's keep the focus on the group, not on me. Not this time.

And one month could become two, then three, and one day, I'd be worthy and strong enough to have a relationship with Bryce.

After the meeting, I found myself easing into the old ritual of mingling. Spotting Charles, I waved him over to where Kevin stood. "Charles, meet Kevin, my sponsor," I said.

They shook hands, and I could see Charles was nervous, and that was my fault for putting the fear of mentioning the lottery in him. I sniggered at the thought, and Charles shot me a frustrated, but fond glance.

"My brother is an asshole," he murmured, and we were on an even keel.

Kevin grinned. "I'm working on converting him to baseball over hockey," he declared with a chuckle.

Charles raised an eyebrow, looking at me. "Baseball? Really, Mikey?"

I gave a half-smile. "Well, he's trying. Says there's more strategy to it than hockey." Charles and I exchanged no-fucking-way glances.

Kevin nodded with enthusiasm. "Exactly! It's all about the long game, strategy over brute force."

Charles laughed, I smiled, and Kevin tried to make his way through a stale donut. The banter was light, easy, and I felt a warmth at being the butt of their jokes as they joined forces to tease me—a warmth that had everything to do with finding my way in this weird new world I'd landed in.

MY ONE-MONTH CHIP BECAME TWO, THEN THREE AND I was close to completing my community service.

The threats from Looper were still coming, but I'd trained myself not to react when I received the texts. As long as Looper and his heavies stayed over on his side and kept it to threats and no action, then I could keep my head buried in the sand.

And I stayed away from Bryce, not wanting to rock the boat, not wanting to scare him away.

Or scare myself.

Then, as spring slowly became summer, I felt stronger inside each day, and the itch of wanting to bet against life shifted into something different without me even noticing. Through all of it—learning to be part of my family again, trying my hardest to show people I'd changed, and reconnecting with friends—my affection and trust in Bryce never wavered.

The warnings still came, but they'd slowed down, one a week, notes in the post had defaulted to just texting now, all garbage and empty threats, and were so infrequent I could forget.

On Midsummer Day, with my sentence down to a

handful of hours to finish before the weird-ass summer fair thing the community garden did each year, I was excited, mindful, and ready to start the rest of my life.

I would always be a recovering addict, but I would fight this every day. I wanted to make amends for real, and see how this growing love for nature, and for the garden, could heal me.

But most of all, I wanted to kiss Bryce again and see where this thing we had between us could go.

Chapter 14

Bryce

I HAD NEVER BEEN SO HAPPY TO SIGN OFF ON A community service form in my life.

Even when Jimmy "The Hippo" Jenkins had left, and he had taken several flats of seedlings with him to dispense to those who he felt needed to enjoy gardening *or else*.

Yeah, sometimes garden time didn't quite smooth out all the wrinkles in a person. I was sure Michael's time spent with us had, if nothing else, given him a hand in discovering himself, his flaws, and his strengths. He'd progressed so well, and now, I was putting my John Hancock on his paperwork. He had done his hours with honors. And I was not commending him simply because we had a maybe romance brewing. He'd earned all the praise. He'd suffered through so much here. Sore backs, bee stings, smashed insects on his fingers, birds pooping on his head, pointed comments from gardeners and visitors. The list was endless, yet he'd persevered, his softer inner side coming to the fore the longer he was here.

I stared down at the paper that would give him his freedom from the San Pedro St. Community Garden. If he ever came back, it was his call to make. I hoped he would. I longed to spend time with him now that we were on an even footing. His call to step back after my desert quest as Leo called it had been the right one. I'd known it as soon as he turned down my offer to stay. I shouldn't have even asked, but I was feeling vulnerable still and, well, I'd wanted someone to hold me through the night.

"Dad, are you coming?! The sun is setting, and we need more herbs!" Leo burst into my office in full summer solstice gear. He was a druid with green robes, paper horns on his head, and bare feet. Good thing his mother couldn't see him thundering about with no shoes.

"I am, yes, is everyone gathered at the altar?" I folded Michael's paper of independence from weeding in half, then tucked it into the pocket of my golden bathrobe. I was the sun, complete with a huge golden cardboard headpiece that Leo and I had made last night. Gold glitter covered everything within a one-mile radius. I had glitter in places a man should never have, but my son was happy, and that was all that mattered.

The robe was a thrift shop find. My feet were also

bare, and I hoped neither of us would step on something pokey and end up in the ER getting tetanus shots.

"Mostly. Michael isn't here yet, but Mrs. Cho is telling people what to do," Leo said, then shoved his horns out of his eyes.

"Okay, let's get to welcoming summer," I said, then led the lad out into the garden. People were gathered in the center, all in various costumes ranging from elves to wizards to Vikings. Not rampaging Vikings, nice ones with packets of fresh herbs for those who wished to partake in the "ritual" about to take place. Mrs. Cho stood in the center of the garden, next to a flower-covered trellis, in her pink unicorn costume. I didn't dare ask what a unicorn had to do with the solstice, but this whole celebration of the garden had been her idea way back, then so I went with the flow.

"There you are!" the tiny unicorn said as I neared her. "We're all ready for the invocation to the earth." She slapped a thick bundle of sage, basil, and oregano into my sunny chest. A cloud of gold glitter drifted upward. We both coughed. "You got enough of that crap sprinkled on you?"

"Leo wanted to make sure I was golden enough," I whispered, then turned to the crowd of local gardeners and the unsheltered who were watching from the gate. I had tried to get them to enter, but the few on the sidewalk seemed uneasy to come in for some reason. That was when I saw the biggest bee I had ever seen walk through the gate. Michael stopped just a few feet inside, gazed in wonder at the gathering, then chuckled. His bee suit was round and fuzzy with a big plastic stinger that swayed when he walked. On his head were springy antenna, and he had painted his face bright yellow. His arms were bare, also yellow, but on his hands were oversized white gloves.

"Dad, Michael is here!" Leo shouted as he darted to the hockey player to drag him to the center spoke. "He's a drone. Boy bees are drones, right, Dad?"

"That's right. Glad you could make it," I said as I offered Michael my hand. I longed to offer him more, but that was a topic for later discussion. We shook, his fingers holding mine a bit longer than most would deem acceptable, but who cared what most thought? "We're about to start. Please, place your herbs on the altar."

He gave me a wink, stepped up to the folding table covered with a white paper tablecloth as well as mounds of herbs, vegetables, and bouquets of flowers. Several of my bees were checking out the flowers on their final trip to the hive for the night. He placed a handful of parsley on the table, bowed with theatrical flair to the setting sun, and inadvertently stung Mrs. Cho with his big stinger. We all had a chuckle over that before I led a small blessing over the offerings. It was something Mrs. Cho had written, and it was the same as every year, but it *meant* something.

"This day, when the sun is at its strongest, we give

our thanks to the bounty given to us by Mother Earth. We will dance on the warm soil as we celebrate the longest day of the year. Blessed be!"

Everyone murmured "blessed be," and then, the dancing began after the offerings to the sun had been gathered and handed out to those who needed them most. The unsheltered thanked us as they moved away, eager to get off the street before the city workers began rousting them for loitering. I'd had a few discussions with the LAPD about what constituted loitering. Gathering with friends was not loitering, I would argue—then was told to mind my tomatoes and let the police mind upholding the law.

"Hey." I spun from watching my friends drifting into the shadows as the night crept over the City of Angels. Michael stood behind me, his stinger now in his hand. I glanced at it, then back to his handsome face. "To avoid any more accidental stings."

"You're a very wise drone," I said, waving goodbye to the last of the local gardeners and a few girl scouts who had wanted to attend. "I have something for you."

Mrs. Cho and Leo were chatting away as they broke down the offering table. I reached around my back, then pulled his paperwork free. The oldies playlist I'd chosen for the dancing was still playing, Little Richard's "Tutti Frutti" filling the garden with rock & roll. A streetlight buzzed into illumination above us as he opened the paper, then read it over.

"Thanks." He slapped his palm with the paper,

before his eyes met mine. "So, I'm now free to date whomever I wish. I mean… if that person wishes to date me, obviously."

"Obviously." I reached down to scratch my belly. Glitter was very itchy. I wondered if my hair would ever be free of the stuff.

He huffed in that way he did that made me chuckle, but I remained silent. I needed to know that he was now ready for this thing we'd somehow managed to put on the back burner to be moved to a hotter flame.

"So, dating."

"It's a lovely way to spend an evening," I remarked as my son and Mrs. Cho began chasing each other around the garden with wilted sprigs of peppermint. Not sure what the game was, but they were enjoying themselves, so peace be with them.

"Bryce, you're acting incredibly weird right now."

"Am I?"

He poked me with his stinger in the belly. That made me laugh. "Okay, I'll stop being weird. Dating. I would very much like to invite you to a midnight meal here in the garden this evening, if you're not going to be busy checking out someone else's hive?"

"I'm a king bee, baby."

"No such thing, but A for effort. Or should that be E for effort. That always confused me." I tapped my chin.

"Oh my god. You're so weird. Insect royal monikers aside, I am not going to be buzzing around anyone else's hive or flower. A midnight meal sounds romantic?"

"I have Leo until Friday," I pointed out just as my son charged past, giggling, with a spry Korean unicorn in hot pursuit. They both reeked of peppermint, which, given how the boy smelled sometimes was okay by me. Mrs. Cho skidded to a halt and tossed back her floppy stuffed horn.

"So, you two are finally going to bump uglies. Good. Leo can stay with me. Go get your freaky-deaky on." We both gaped at her. "What? You two think I'm blind just because I'm old?" She waved a hoof in our face, then called out to Leo to grab his shoes and that he was going to sleep over at her place. He hooted in glee. Mrs. Cho had that amazing cat, lots of sugary food, and old DVDs of martial arts movies that Courtney would birth a rhino over if she knew her baby boy was watching.

"Hey, no bloody Shaolin master flicks!" I called out, but assumed my request would be ignored by the bossy unicorn. I sighed, knowing Leo would be kung fu fighting everyone and their beagle tomorrow, then brought my attention back to the sexiest bee this side of the hives. "They will so be watching *Mad Monkey Kung Fu;* I just know it."

"A little roundhouse to the chops never hurt anyone," he tossed out.

"Said by someone who has never had his ass chewed out by his ex-wife," I replied, then rubbed at my belly a bit more. "I'd like to go home and shower first, but if you're up for a late dinner, we could come here or—"

"Why don't you come to my place this time?"

"Sure. That would be nice. Do you have food?" I asked as I herded my son and my landlady out the gate before locking it tightly.

"We'll pick something up along the way," he said.

I nodded. The four of us walked back to our little row house, Leo darting forward, then racing back to us, hyped up on strawberries, I guess? Who knew what was fueling him, but as we stood at Mrs. Cho's door, I took a moment to kneel down and take him by his shoulders.

"Okay, I need you to chill out a little bit, okay? I know it's been an exciting night, but Mrs. Cho isn't a young woman anymore."

"I heard that. I'm standing right here," Mrs. Cho sniffed. Michael turned his head to hide his smirk. "You're as old as you feel."

"Yes, of course," I hurried to amend. "Mrs. Cho is a young woman who is not used to chasing after a boy— so please try to settle down a little. And please, do not pester Lefty too much."

"I'll be good, I promise. Mrs. Cho is a good babysitter," he said as he beamed up at her. She ruffled his already chaotic hair.

"I know. She has my phone number, so if anything—"

"Oh, for the love of peanut logs would you just go

get kissy-faced?" Mrs. Cho huffed, took Leo by the hand, and led him into her apartment. Lefty could be heard meowing his hello as I knelt there staring at the door she'd shut in my face, then rose. "Guess we're going to go get our kissy faces on. Give me ten minutes?"

"Sure." We climbed the stairs. I felt his stare on my sunny backside, so made sure to swing my beams just a tad more than usual. "You get that sunbeam any closer to my face, I'm going to have sunstroke."

We were chuckling as we entered my apartment. "So where exactly is your place? I assume it's not near here." I asked, yanking my sunny cardboard back piece off as I crossed the living room. My robe caught on the spiked ends, lifting it to bare my back. Thankfully I had briefs on, or Michael would have been flashed.

I never heard him coming up behind me. I thought a man that large would be louder. His arms snaked around my middle, pulling me to a halt. His groin brushed my ass. Even with his bee suit between us, something hot and vibrant unfurled in my belly. I reached to hold him tighter, my heart rate spiking when he lowered his lips to my neck. Then, he drew back, spitting out what I assumed was glitter.

"Oh shit, sorry. I need to shower," I said as I lingered in his arms.

"I want to join you so badly, but I also want to spend time getting to know you.

His lips were beside my ear, each word a warm puff

sending blood rushing to my cock. "Rushing into anything seems foolish."

"Tell me you've been to group without telling me you've been to group," I sighed out, pulling myself from his embrace before turning to gaze at him. "We should take this slow… I agree. Impulsive decisions always come back to bite a person in the ass."

He reached up to brush something from beside my left eye. "Glob of glitter," he whispered before stealing a light kiss, then stepping back from me. "Go shower. I'm going to jog in place while reciting the Storm faceoff wins versus losses stats to keep me from thinking about you being wet and naked just behind that door."

Unable to say anything other than "take me," I bumbled my way into the cramped bath, closed the door on temptation, and peeled off my clothes with haste—my dick stiff as a fire poker. I blew out a breath, pushed at my cock with a finger, then stepped into the shower. Perhaps, I needed to flick the fucking thing like nurses used to do in the old days when men got hard-ons during a sponge bath. Although, a flick might make it more ready. It had been a long time for me. Far too long if I were being frank.

I ignored my prick the best I could, waffling between cranking the hot water to dim its desire and just jerking off. And while tugging one off had its merits, I wanted to wait. Now that Michael and I were freed from any ethical line one or both of us might cross by accident, I wanted his touch to be the next thing my cock felt. Or his mouth. Or the heat of his body as I sank into him.

Right, that was not helping. I lathered, shampooed, then rinsed in the coldest water I could handle. My dick not only shrank, it crawled into my body to avoid the icy fingers peppering it. Shivering, I dried myself—glad to see only a few sparkles of gold could be seen in my hair and stubble where I hadn't shaved in a few days—then exited the bath with a towel around my waist.

Michael was sipping coffee, his stinger resting on the counter, his eyes locking onto me as a cheetah would a vulnerable gazelle. My once-hidden dick climbed out of its safe little space with speed. Damn it. Behaving myself was not going to be easy if he kept looking at me as if I were a garden buffet salad bar.

"You look good in that towel," he offered into his mug. "Damn it. Nix that. I'm not going to say another thing about how sexy you are when you're damp. Shit. You know what?" He placed his mug on the counter, picked up his stinger, and walked to the door. "You get dressed. I'll be in the foyer poking myself repeatedly with my stinger."

I roared.

He gave me a playful wink, then exited, muttering "ouch, ouch, ouch" all the way down the stairs.

Chapter 15

Michael

WE PICKED UP PIZZA, NOTHING SPECIAL, BUT MY stomach grumbled, and we did this whole exchanging of glances and smiles thing that made my heart expand.

There was a reason I wanted him back at my place tonight—so he could understand how low I'd fallen and see what I had left.

I wasn't a millionaire. I was just me.

I didn't think at this time that we'd run into anyone, but just my luck there was Charles on the patio, nursing a beer and staring at us.

"Mikey," he murmured. "Bryce."

"Hi." Bryce was polite and attempted to untangle our fingers, but I tightened my hold.

There was an awkward moment where we all stared at each other, but for once, Charles wasn't teasing, or asking if I was okay, or even freaking smiling that positive smile he always had going on.

Dread gripped me—what had happened? Had I done something? Was he going to ask me to leave? Or shit, what if this was worse? Were Clare and the kids okay?

"CZee? What's wrong?" I said, reverting to the childhood nickname I had for him, something that I hadn't used since my jealousy, temper, and all around failures had driven a wedge between us.

I'd forgotten that connection... that familiarity. I'd grown bitter that I was always going to be second in everything and look how wrong I'd been.

I took a step toward him, tugging Bryce with me.

"Storm management," Charles muttered, and placed the beer on the table. "It's all good, Mikey." His voice was a little slurred, and I wondered how many of those beers he'd consumed.

"What about them?"

"Nothing you need to worry about," he answered with a sigh, and something about that sigh made me want to fix something for my big brother. The Storm had finished outside a place for the playoffs, middle of the group, not even scraping a wildcard, but so close it must have hurt.

That was what I'd said when the season ended, when Charles and his little family had headed off on vacation. I'd handed over all the platitudes, said I understood the loss, but deep down, somehow, hockey had become less of a thing for me.

It had lost its importance.

And in doing so, maybe Charles had lost his

sounding board in me? As an alternate captain, me, him, and the other alternate, Prez, had always dissected the losses, the pain, the wins, the highs, and he'd lost that.

Lost me.

"I'm sorry I wasn't there for you. If I'd been on the ice, we could have gotten a win," I blurted, feeling out of place and hot all over.

Charles glanced up, then let out a derisive snort. "And there it is, the arrogance that your presence meant we'd be fixed, and would have won everything."

That stung, and worse, Bryce, probably sensing the gravity of the moment between Charles and me, unlaced our fingers and stepped back, giving us room. I glanced at him, and he gave me a quick smile that reassured me he wasn't leaving, then strolled off to examine the undergrowth in the shadows. I fought the hurt that Charles still thought I was arrogant, then it hit me that, maybe, I was handling the addiction as best as I could, but that didn't mean I was a nice person. I was a shitty, hurtful asshole, and what if that was all I'd ever be?

"I know I'm fucked up and—"

"No. Stop," Charles interrupted, then drew a deep breath. "Sorry. Fuck. Just ignore me." He waved at where Bryce had gone. "Don't leave your man hanging."

I held up a hand, jogged to where Bryce was and pressed the key to the pool house in his hand. "Give me a while?" I asked, hoping he wouldn't leave, but understanding if that was what he had to do. He didn't hesitate, smiled, and a fleck of glitter in his hair sparkled in the low lighting, then he touched my arm.

"Take your time. Family is a priority in *all* things."

I watched him leave, after pointing him in the right direction, and then, went straight back to my brother, who was still sitting in the same place, staring mournfully at the darkened yard beyond. I scraped a chair as I sat down and startled him.

"What are you doing?" He sounded shocked I'd come back.

"You look sad." I didn't know how else to say it.

"I do *not* look sad," he defended, then frowned. "And I don't need sympathy."

I shrugged. "I wasn't going to offer you sympathy. I want to apologize because I'm sorry for whatever I did or said, and I only wanted to explain why I feel—"

"Not this bullshit again. You do realize that not everything is about you, right?"

I was so confused. "But sometimes it *is* about me, and what I did and—"

"Isn't that what you accused Prez of thinking that day?"

"What?"

"That everything was about him? And you told him to fuck off."

"I didn't exactly…" I stopped. Yes, I had said that to Prez, thrown away his support and his understanding, not given him a chance to talk. But, since then, consumed with guilt at first, and then hope that one day we could be friends again without all the bullshit, I'd broken down all the hurtful pieces of me and tried to remake them into something better.

"What did Storm management say?" I said, ignoring the fact that it was clear my big brother wanted an argument, a way of releasing the tension I could see in every line of him.

"That their captain fucked up," he said, then chuckled, but it was a dark and hard sound.

I frowned. "Bullshit," I said with loyal determination. "It's not all on you."

"But you *have* to defend me; you're my brother."

I leaned forward in my chair, determined to have my say. "Bull. Shit," I said in a soft tone.

For a moment, he was startled, then subsided, the beer resting on his belly, and he gave the appearance of being defeated. That wasn't like Charles; he was positive and focused, and losses rolled off him like water off a duck's back.

So, I forged ahead with my train of thought because, maybe, he needed someone to tell him how good he was. I'd always thought it was me who deserved the praise, the orphan with no family, pulled in from a home, given a life they didn't ask for. I'd battled the newness of it all, the fact these people were strangers, and I'd deserved to be held up as a hero.

What did that leave for Charles? Did anyone tell him how much he'd battled and how great he was? I've never known a man like him, a brother who loved me, my family despite us not being blood related. Maybe I needed to step up and give him the praise he deserved, or at least get him to see he wasn't to blame in the way the Storm had played.

"The team had a bad year," I began with so much caution he winced. I sounded like an idiot, so I pulled up my pants and pushed ahead. Yes, they'd struggled, but jeez, they'd fought hard. "It wasn't your year, and let's be honest, they've had to fight all the shit about me as well. I don't just mean me being thrown off the team and what they might have lost with that, and I don't mean to sound arrogant, but I was part of that team, and it's on me that I fucked up everything for them. All the gossip, and the media shit, and the lies." I huffed a laugh. "And the truths. You had to deal with all of the hockey side, with a side order of your brother ruining his life."

Charles started defensively, but then sighed. "Yeah, maybe. If I'm completely honest…" He scrubbed his eyes. "Maybe, sometimes, I've been off my game, and maybe it was your fault, or mine for not being able to process everything. Or the guilt that I didn't notice sooner."

I growled. "Jeez—"

"No, let me talk. You are a power winger, an alternate, and a big fucking loss to the team." He glanced at me.

I waited for that moment where I should feel pride

163

on hearing that the team missed my skills, but sadness consumed me I'd even thought that in the first place. God my head is messed up.

Charles continued. "I'm the captain, and I'm supposed to be able to handle all of this, ignore my personal life when I'm on the ice, pull back the wins. That's the job."

He was carrying the weight of the season's failures on his shoulders, as well as worrying about me.

"Hey, you've done more than anyone could've asked for," I said. "This season's been rough, but you've led the team the best way anyone could. Don't shoulder all this alone." I meant every word, hoping to lift some of the burden he carried as our team's leader. "You're a great captain, Charles."

"The league tables say otherwise." He stopped, as if he needed a moment to think, and then he sighed. "I know Management called you."

"Oh."

"You never told me."

"It's complicated."

"But they asked you about coming back to the team?"

"Kind of," I hedged, recalling that I'd never really thought through their offer with the shed fire and all. In fact, I'd pushed it right back and ignored it, which was unhealthy.

"In what capacity?" Charles asked, and I knew what he meant. Would I be coming back at four mill a year, would I be an alternate, would the last year be written off as never happening? After all, I'd done everything they said I should, served my time, done my best to be a better man, but that didn't mean I deserved a goddamn reward.

"They didn't say much, just that they weren't averse to me returning. Their words, not mine."

He snorted a laugh. "Well, I'm not averse to you coming back."

"What about the rest of the guys?"

He shot me a glance. "It's split. You know I have your back, and Prez, and Cam, unequivocally. We get it. Some of the other guys, the ones who know you, they're okay. But the new kids, I don't know." He straightened, then crossed his arms over his chest. "But I'm captain, and I'll do what is best for the team. If you come back, maybe it's right, maybe it's wrong, but the team comes first." He was daring me to argue, but I felt the same way. No point in my skating again at NHL level when all I did was drag down morale or made things difficult for everyone. A small part of me never wanted to play hockey again.

The rest of me missed it so bad I thought I'd die.

"That's a damn fine hero pose, big brother?" I teased, and he rolled his eyes, making me laugh. "I always knew, growing up, that you'd be a captain one day, always knew I'd be second to you."

He tensed, then shook his head. "No, you don't get it, Mikey. You were never just my second. You're my brother, my alternate captain; we've always made each other stronger." His words hit me deep, a reminder of our bond beyond the ice. "I miss you out there, and I've loved you since the day Mom and Dad brought you home. You were so happy to be hugged…" He pressed a hand to his chest. "Since you joined the Storm, I lost that in you, and I missed my brother… in here."

Tears spilled from my eyes, and in a flurry of motion, we were up and hugging each other for the longest time.

"Will you come back?" he asked me, his face buried in my hair. "If they ask you?"

I extricated myself.. "Did they tell you they wanted me, as well?" Hope flared in my chest, then doubts stifled that moment of joy. "I don't know if…"

"You're right—they want to test the market, the fans, see what the feelings are out there about you coming back, but the target on your back…" He gripped my arm. "I won't lose you to the addictions again." He was determined and focused.

I was here tonight taking a first step into what I wanted my life to be—settled, focused, and with Bryce in the middle of it all. I was due to start volunteering with the Honor Guards veterans' team in September, all that stuff about repaying the NHL and making myself look good with a view to getting back on the Storm… Did I want Storm hockey?

Did hockey want me?

Going back to the team would go a long way to paying off the debts no one knew about, but what if the Storm paid me next to nothing because they were just trying me out, and then, I would never be able to clear any of it.

Today, at the celebration, the latest note had been left pinned to the fence outside the secret garden again. *500. Each day. Tick Tock.*

I couldn't even clear one day with the money Charles put in my account. Let alone five hundred a day.

Charles softened. "Your absence was felt, but it's on all of us to step up, and we could be there for you, but… I worry."

I covered his hand on my arm and squeezed. "One step at a time."

That was all I could give him.

It was all I could give anyone.

We hugged again, and Charles went back into the house. I gave myself a few moments of settling my thoughts, then went to find Bryce. Only, as I approached the pool house, I found him sitting on the low wall outside, his head tilted up to the sky.

"Why didn't you go in?" I asked.

Bryce glanced over at me, a half-smile on his face. "This is your place. I wanted you to show me."

Nodding, I led him inside. The pool house was small, almost claustrophobic compared to what I used to call home.

167

"Charles offered me a room in the main house, but I refused."

"You needed your space."

"Yep, also I was defiant and pissed and…" I chuckled. "I needed this to remind me of what I'd lost."

I gave him the guided tour. We bumped into each other as we tried to take it in turns checking out the small bathroom and the tiny kitchen, and the huge sofa taking up most of the space along with the TV on the wall.

"And this is the bedroom," I said, gesturing inside, and waiting for him to see it. There was a large bed, bigger than a double, no room on either side for a cabinet, but a unit at the end and a closet in one corner opposite.

"Cozy," he said and reached for my hand, but I avoided him, cautious, and sat on the far end of the sofa. He sent me a puzzled glance but waited with all his Bryce-like patience.

"The house I lost had six bedrooms, five bathrooms. I had a pool like Charles does, and a hot tub, and I earned a shit ton of money. I could afford anything I wanted, had the entire kitchen redone just because I could." I left out the pain of living on my own, in a place where gambling was as easy as breathing.

"Well, I like it here," Bryce defended and shuffled a little closer to me on the sofa.

I glanced around me. "This is all that I'm worth, and

it's not even mine," I said, and hated the small voice I used.

He had to know I didn't have anything.

"Your worth isn't in what you own, but who you are," Bryce muttered, his eyes flaring. "And you are a good man, Michael Zhang."

"I'm jealous, and angry, and my self-esteem is for shit," I defended, then realized this was not the best way of me leading the evening where I wanted it to go. I wanted to kiss Bryce, I wanted to lose myself in his arms, and learn all the parts of him I didn't know yet. I wanted to kiss thank-yous on his skin, take him into my mouth, I wanted…

I wanted *all* of him.

The smiles and the encouragement, and the cute thing he had with his bees, and his secret garden, and the way he looked at me right now.

As if he wanted to consume me whole.

Listing all my bad points wasn't going to achieve any of that.

"I'm very good at blow jobs," I blurted, and he stifled laughter so that it bubbled up as this weird high-pitched snort. I got super defensive. "I am." I met his gaze.

"Why don't you come here?" he asked softly.

"We're doing this?" I asked, already hard, already forgetting any hint of doubt.

"We're doing this."

I'd never moved so fast.

Chapter 16

Bryce

IT WAS FUNNY IN A WAY. NOW WE WERE HERE, ALONE, with the fires of passion flaring, I felt a little trepidation.

I always liked to think I was a kind and experienced lover. My ex had never had complaints until I was too stoned to perform. Our marital bed became a battlefield, which did not lend itself to stellar sexual performances. Then, I'd gone months without any contact as I worked my way through rehab. Michael had been right to pull the brake on us earlier because addicts were inclined to swap one addiction for another. I wouldn't been with anyone for a long, long time. Not someone who meant anything to me, and god knows, Michael had come to mean a great deal to me. Would I be able to please him? What if I couldn't? What if he left his bed disappointed and disillusioned like—

"Hey, are you still with me?" His voice shattered the wall of worry I'd been erecting.

I blinked, smiled nervously, then melted back into his embrace. "Sorry, I was letting my inner saboteur take over." I nestled closer, allowing my hands to roam over his shoulders.

"I know that voice really well. Dude sucks," he said as the smell of jasmine floated into the pool house via the screen door.

"Yeah, he does. So, where were we?"

"If my old man memory serves, we were right here." I cupped his face and stole a soft kiss. It was sweet as candy. But like candy, it was too tempting to stop at only one taste.

He met me for another kiss with a bit more fire, his hands sliding around my waist, under my shirt, to caress my lower back. Eager for more sugar, I licked into his mouth. His tongue slid over mine as he moved a step to the left. A mere fraction of an inch. The rub of stiff cock over stiff cock blasted the suggestion of going slow to bits. TNT had nothing on the explosive, concussive force of erection meeting erection.

We both gasped, pulling cool air into our mouths before our hunger overtook us. We had been too long denying our yearning for each other. He nipped at my lower lip as my touch roamed over his chest, finding, then tugging on, the buttons of his shirt. If some went flying, I'd sew them on for him free of charge tomorrow. Right now, I needed flesh under my palms.

"Get this off," he grunted, yanking at my shirt. I yipped when the collar got stuck on the small earrings in my lobe. "Oh fuck, sorry." He eased the material off, then kissed the offended earlobe. A shudder of molten lava raced through me. My head fell back, then to the side, as I offered myself up to him as if he were a ravenous vampire, and I was his willing meal. Which was kind of on the mark. He could eat me up, and I wouldn't whimper once in protest.

"Oh shit," I moaned when he sucked that lobe, using his tongue to wiggle the small rings back and forth as his hands slithered from my back down to my ass. His hands were large, his grip firm. I ground my hips into him, clinging now to his shoulders as he massaged my backside as if it was buttermilk biscuit dough. "Michael, this is…"

"Yeah, it is." He nibbled along my jugular, then swept me off my feet with a soft grunt. I wasn't a small man, but he seemed to handle me with ease. We fell onto the bed with such force the tasteful padded headboard slammed into the wall. "Fuck. Why did we wait so long?"

His lips trailed down my chest, then latched onto a nipple. I replied in some sort of language that might have been Greek. My cock was leaking now, ready, and willing to fire off at the merest touch. His teeth found the hard nub. I cried out. He licked it better before palming my cock through my pants.

"Hair… trigger," I warned, trying my best to free

him from his belt so we could get that nice fat cock of his freed and in my hand, mouth, or ass. I wasn't picky. Maybe all three. "So close…"

"Yeah, I know. I'll get your mind off that," he promised, lifting his head from my aching nipple to wink at me. Yep, that there was the wink of a succubus if I ever saw one. There was a sensual difference in our skin tones, Michael's pale skin next to my tan flesh was a definite turn-on. And god, he had so many freckles, and I wanted to taste every one of them.

He worked my cock for a moment, until I was writhing and whimpering, and then, he eased off me. Lifting his weight from my belly, he unwrapped me just like Leo did his Christmas presents. Socks, briefs, and pants went flying, and my unease returned. I was not an athlete like he was. My body was lean, too lean according to Mrs. Cho, who was trying to fatten me up with bowls of gimbap, bingsu, and—

"Where do you keep going?" he asked, lapping around my prick, using the tip of his tongue to gather the pre-cum collecting there.

"I'm here. I just… my mind kind of… god you look so hot with my dick resting on your lip." He smiled sinfully, his hands holding my calves now, easing my legs open wider. "I'm not as beautiful as you. And I'm several years older than you. I've got scars and—"

"Hey, you know what? I have scars too. And trust me, Bryce, you're way more beautiful than I am. I'm not really all that."

"I disagree. You're all that and a can of… Fuck!" I groaned when his lips sucked my cockhead. Just the head, and just a quick suck before he pulled off with a *pop,* then began easing my legs upward. How was that getting my mind off of blowing a nut?

"Do you want to show me that hole of yours?"

I managed to squeak out a sound that could have been a yes, then pulled my thighs to my chest, sweat on my brow. Grasping my thighs—thank all the heavens I did yoga, so this position was easy for me—I let my head rest on the puffy pillows that had been tossed about when he'd gotten out of bed this morning. Michael was not a bedmaker; that I had learned this evening. Another thing I learned was that he was not shy in bed, asking for exactly what he wanted was such a turn-on to me. He bowed his head, wriggling on the mattress, and sucked at my balls until I was a puddle of goo.

"Pretty man," he cooed, pressing his tongue flat to my taint, then sliding it to my waiting hole. A gurgle of pleasure bubbled out of me. He went to work, pressing the tip of his tongue into me, using his fingers to open me even wider, then sliding a digit in. Moans filled the room as he brought me to the very edge, then sat back on his heels. Chin coated with spittle while his short hair was sodden with sweat. "Delicious man," he added before swiping the back of his hand over his lips. "Say it." He cupped my balls. "Say how pretty you are. Tell me how good your ass tastes. Say it, Bryce."

"Asshole," I ground out in a short, rough laugh. "My ass tastes divine. My body is an artwork. There, now it's my turn."

He chuckled as he let me manhandle him into the mattress. He could have tossed me off at any time, but he spread himself out, legs akimbo, arms up over his head, to allow me to feast on his body. And I did. I kissed him hard on the mouth, then repeated his touch, teasing his dark nipples, then lower, finding so many freckles on my way down to my goal, his cock. His prick kicked as I took it in hand. I laved a long stripe from tip to base. Over and over and over until he was cursing my ancestors for having a cocktease like me in the family tree.

My mouth closed over his shaft, taking him in just an inch, then easing off. The strong muscles in his legs tightened. I held them to the bed, enjoying the crisp crackle of dark-red hair beneath my palms. I brought him close several times, taking him to the root, then pulling off when he would begin to thrust. Finally, he began to waver.

"Close?" I asked, flicking the purplish head of his dick. He was soaked now, his chest heaving, his fingers latched onto the sides of the mattress in a death grip.

"Yes, close..." he huffed between ragged breaths.

"Tell me you're worth everything. Say it, and I will climb on you and ride you like the motherfucking stallion that you are. Tell me that you are a good man with a loving heart. Say that and paradise is yours."

"You think your ass is paradise?"

"I do." I kneeled between his thighs. I was tempted to take his balls into my mouth, but knew he was balancing on a thin wire. I wanted him to come while he was inside me. This time.

"Nice." He closed his eyes as if in pain. "I'm a good man." His eyelids flew open. "Now get on my dick."

"With pleasure." I shimmied up, stole a hot, wet kiss, then stalled.

"Box under the bed. Skate box." He played my ass like a damn bongo as I lay down to fetch the necessities.

Once I was back on his thighs, his grin was playful demon seduction. It made me sizzle inside. "Yeah, there you go." I fished out a condom and some lube, eyeballing the prostate massager. "We'll use that later. Right now, all I want in your ass is my cock."

"Your tongue was there," he mentioned while rolling a condom over his fat prick.

"Yeah, and my dick is jealous. Lots of lube. Finger it up into yourself deep."

"God, you are so bossy." I rushed to coat my fingers, then eased them into myself. His eyes were hot as coals, his hands tickling over my sides and belly. When I was pleased with the slip and slide, I shifted up, bracing his head with my hands, staring into each other's eyes, as I moved, stretching up into a puppy pose of sorts. His prick would graze my hole, then slide over it, teasing and tempting both of us.

"Bryce, I'm this close to throwing you on your back," he warned.

"And that would be bad how?" I asked, then levered myself into position, the pressure on my hole growing as I pushed back inch by inch. The stretch burned. It had been ages since I'd sat on a cock, let alone one this big. I loved every moment. He guided me, fingers biting into my hips, his jaw set, and I focused on a trio of tiny freckles near his nipple, trying to think about anything other than the pain and ecstasy.

"So tight," he forced out through gritted teeth as I took more and more. Midway, I had to pause to catch my breath and let that burn ease. "Go slow." I nodded, forcing breaths out through my nose as if I were giving birth. "But not too slow."

That made me snort. He moaned. I shivered. The tension as I eased him all the way in was divine, but the fullness when he bottomed out was earth shattering. I felt as if I couldn't draw a breath. He rolled his hips. Stars exploded all around me.

"Move baby," he whispered, his fingers now biting hard.

I eased up, then down, the surge of pleasure winded me. His thighs quaked as I began to catch a rhythm, not a smooth one, no, but a sloppy wild one that had us both crying out into the night as our bodies collided time and again.

He released my hip, using his free hand to grab my bobbing cock. One stroke. That was all it took to bring me to climax. My head fell back, and I howled like the coyotes I'd heard on the dunes in the dead of night. Cum spurted out of me, coating his hand and belly, the pearly droplets clinging to the hair on his abdomen. He stiffened, his eyes wide as he rutted into me, filling the condom with surge after surge of hot spend. My body was a trembling mass. Arms weak, legs rubbery, cock spewing madly.

"Give me every drop," Michael growled, milking me with strong strokes until it became too much, and I fell forward, his slick fingers easing away from my prick.

I lifted my head from his shoulder. Our dreamy gazes met as he eased two spunk-coated fingers into his mouth. The sight was perhaps the most erotic thing I had ever witnessed. When he removed those digits, I captured his mouth with mine, sweeping in deep to pick up, then mingle, my taste around.

"Fuck, you're delicious," he repeated the same words from earlier.

"Yeah, I really am," I concurred, which got me a smile that could melt ice caps, then a tender pat on the backside. With great care for my ass, which was already starting to voice its complaints about such a big shaft in such a tiny hole, I fell off him to the bed, my leg resting over his thigh, my arm on his chest. He found his breath much faster than I did, damned athletes. Boneless, I let him shift me around, easing out from under me to pad to a small bathroom off the bedroom.

The night air trickled in, caressing my overheated skin as he splashed about in the sink.

He returned as I battled to keep my eyes open. I rolled to my back from my side, taking the warm cloth he had brought. He sat beside me, watching me clean myself, his face shadowed in the muted lights from the lone lamp on the other side of the bed.

"Can you stay?" he asked, making me feel a myriad of emotions. All of them rosy, romantic, and rapturous.

Should I? Could I? Dare I?

Yes, yes I did dare. And I should, and I could, and I would.

"Yes, I'll stay."

Chapter 17

Michael

WAKING UP WITH BRYCE, I FELT DIFFERENT. THERE WAS comfort in having someone close. His breathing was steady, and it was calming. It was nice to not be alone, and this was more than a hookup. I had this sense of being grounded—something I hadn't felt in a long time. The physical closeness was comforting, but it was more than that—it was as if the last of my emotional barriers had come down. In his arms, the chaos and noise in my head quieted down, replaced by a feeling of calm and safety.

Bryce was nestled in my arms with his back to me, and I couldn't help but feel a sense of contentment as I touched him and felt the warmth of his skin. "You're so warm," I murmured, half to myself. Bryce hummed in response, a sound of agreement, but I wasn't sure he was awake. In that moment, just between sleep and waking everything felt right, and the thought crossed my mind that I could stay like this forever. If I stayed like this, cocooned in this moment, I would never have to face the world again. The mistakes I'd made, the trail of messes I'd left behind, the secrets I still had, the therapy, the groups… they could all just… disappear.

But that's not reality, is it?

Escaping isn't the same as facing.

"I can hear you thinking," Bryce mumbled, and pushed back against me, my morning erection so happy to be nestled between his ass cheeks. We'd slept naked, warm skin against warm skin, and inhaling the scent of him, I pressed a kiss to his neck and nibbled at his nape as he wriggled.

"Morning breath," he muttered and slid out from my hold, blinking down at me.

"Spare…" I couldn't talk, the sun peeked through the drapes and cast a halo around him, and I was speechless. I'd never seen anyone so beautiful, his soft smile hesitant. I'd waited so long to fall in love, but somehow it had happened despite myself.

"Huh?" he said, and yawned widely, stretching tall, his cock bobbing hello.

I scrambled faster than an Olympic sprinter out of that bed and into my tiny bathroom, delving into the drawer of things kept for Charles' guests.

"Aha!" I announced and waved a new toothbrush at him, scraping at the wrapping and handing it to him as if it were a prize and he'd just won a race. He took it with a smile, and next to each other, in the small space, hips bumping, we brushed our teeth, then took turns to use the bathroom, before coming together in the smallest shower cubicle imaginable.

Bryce and I tried to fit, which was almost comical given we were grown men, and one of us still worked out most days to keep their hockey muscles ready, and the other had a gardener's build with biceps and broad shoulders, and… I needed to stop thinking about how he looked, otherwise we'd never get out of here.

"We need a strategy here," I joked, as we shuffled around awkwardly.

He laughed, and in that tight space, our movements became less about showering and more of an intimate dance. When at last we managed to find a position where we slotted together, our eyes met, the laughter stopped, and we shared a soul-deep kiss—brief, but full of meaning—his hands cupping my face and smoothing my hair from my eyes as the water trickled over us. This wasn't like the four-man shower I'd had in my old house, the one I'd barely used because it was too big, this was ridiculous and cute and so freaking perfect for me.

"This is… cozy," Bryce quipped, his voice warm as we kissed again. I couldn't help but think, despite the cramped quarters, I wouldn't have wanted to be anywhere else.

We managed to wash. We even managed to towel our hair dry, but that was as far as we got, tumbling back into bed, and this time, I wanted to spend time learning every bit of Bryce's body, from his nose to his toes and everything in between. Well, not his toes, that wasn't my thing, but fuck... all the bits in the middle were stopping me from climbing any higher.

When I sucked him down, kissed his balls, nibbled at the insides of his thighs, and had him begging for me to get on with it, I was all too happy to do so, and I swallowed him deep into my throat.

He gripped my shoulders. "Please." That was all he said, but it was enough for me to let him tug me up until I blanketed him, pressed him into the mattress. "Please?" he said again, only this time it was a question.

I kissed him then, gentle, caring, and we slid against each other, so slow, so careful, and when my orgasm hit, it was intense, and I couldn't help myself, I had to tell him how I felt.

He had to know.

"I love you, Bryce," I whispered as he was coming, his back arching, his cock spurting between us.

And he whispered the words right back at me. "I love you."

We dressed at speed, grinning at each other, the knock on the door enough to scare the living daylights out of us both, which meant more secret smiles and snickering.

"Breakfast!" Charles called. "Up at the house!"

"Okay!" I called back because he expected an answer, but it was habit that had me acknowledging what he'd said, as I hadn't set foot in Charles's house since I couldn't remember when.

Since before.

Clare and the girls were in there, and photos on the wall, and kids' art on the refrigerator, and sofas made for curling up and reading bed time stories to Hope and Grace. In that house was everything I didn't deserve.

I think it must have been grief that gripped me, and I stumbled back to the bed, falling as if I couldn't stand anymore, and I hung my head.

"Breathe," Bryce encouraged as I grappled with a sudden panic attack. His calm presence next to me and the soothing stroke on my arm was enough that it anchored me back to reality. "Just breathe," he repeated. "In. Out. In…" His steadiness was a lifeline, pulling me back from the edge of dread. I focused on his voice, tried hard to let it guide my breathing, and bit by bit, the wave of anxiety receded. His simple, steady support had stopped me in my tracks, and I reached blindly for his hand, gripping it, lacing our fingers, and kissing his knuckles, tears pricking my eyes.

"Shit," was about all I could manage.

"Do you need water?" he asked me. At least he wasn't asking me what happened, or why I'd shut down so quick, or wanting answers from me.

"No," I murmured. "I can't… I haven't… it's all the kinds of normal I don't deserve."

"Okay."

He didn't push, and I pressed my lips to his hand again, keeping them there, hunching over. Shouldn't he be telling me that I was being stupid? That I should just walk in there and pretend everything was fine?

I felt shaky, as if I'd worked the hardest shift on ice, my legs like jelly, my breathing harsh, but the spark of something was pulling me back, and I realized Bryce was talking.

"… then I just said: "it's a wheelbarrow, and no one wants to see that."" He chuckled. "Anyway, Leo took the frog out, and apologized to Mrs. Cho, but—"

"Thank you," I interrupted, pressed one last kiss to his hand, then released my hold. "Thank you."

I turned to glance at him, and he smiled. "Always."

"I need to fix my hair," I lied and hid away in the bathroom for a moment, trying not to look at the princess toothbrush he'd used, or see the shower in the mirror. Instead, I stared at my reflection as I rubbed wax on my fingers to warm it. Then, same as every other day, I ruffled my fingers through my hair and whispered my daily affirmations to my reflection.

"My past does not define me. I am more than my addiction. I have the strength to overcome it. My family, friends, and well-being are my priorities, not gambling. Each day I am free from gambling, I gain back a piece of myself. I deserve a life filled with joy, peace, and fulfillment, free from gambling." I swallowed. The last of these was always the hardest.

"My mistakes are lessons, not life sentences. I am learning and growing every day."

When I came out, there was no sign of Bryce, and my heart dropped. I'd gone too far, shown him I wasn't fixed, and he'd run.

I didn't blame him.

But then, I noticed his phone on my bed, the small backpack he'd brought with him, his discarded T-shirt from last night, and the Storm-branded hanger on the bed, my closet open, and I followed the sound of laughter outside.

Which is where I found Bryce, wearing one of my spare Storm jerseys, with my number and my name, chatting to Charles and placing dishes on the garden table under the wide awning, Hope helping by carrying over a basket of rolls.

"Hey bro!" Charles called. "Bryce said we should eat outside!"

Bryce glanced at me and shrugged. "Thought we should take advantage of the LA sunshine. Lotion! Make sure you're covered up!"

All the love inside me just welled, and I kissed him in front of everyone, and when Hope broke us apart with a giggle, I picked her up and whirled her around, then sat down with her on my lap.

She patted me, her tiny hands tracing my face. "You're funny, Uncle Red," she announced.

I felt a hand on my knee. Grace wanted in on the

action, so I scooped her up as well, and bounced my nieces and made them giggle until they couldn't stop.

Then, I ate so much bacon I got accused of stealing it.

Sue me.

Not that they were wrong.

"What are you doing today?" Charles asked as Clare and Bryce cleared up, and we passed plates in through the window.

I had no idea. No plans. No structure. But I knew what I wanted to do.

"I'm going to go to the gardens and help out," I said, and Charles elbowed me in the side.

"Yeah," he said. "I like that for you."

―――――

BRYCE AND I DROVE IN SILENCE BACK TO THE COMMUNITY gardens, but it wasn't a heavy silence, it was peaceful, and it was the first time in so long that I'd felt so quiet in my thoughts. I tried to imagine placing a bet right now, or handling cards, but I didn't get the buzz of anticipation, and I shoved both experimental thoughts away.

I wasn't fixed. I would be an addict forever, but if I could just keep Bryce in my heart, and my family there as well, then maybe, I could have an entire army at my back.

My mistakes are lessons, not life sentences.

The only niggling thing was the text on my phone.

500. Tick Tock. Boston calling.

"Fuck off," I muttered, then deleted it, ignoring the cell. That was not my voice, they didn't have a recording of me, that wasn't me saying I'd throw a game. That wasn't me, pathetic and begging for twenty K.

Not. Me.

"Bad message?" Bryce asked, having no idea that I still had one more secret waiting on the sidelines. I needed to talk to Charles—he was my brother, and he'd clear this debt for me if I asked. But we'd come so far, and I should have been honest earlier, because now could be too late.

I should sound Bryce out about this. I didn't know too much about his addiction, but he must have advice for me, and we loved each other, and he'd never stop loving me.

Right?

"Marketing," I lied, but then I sighed, and he raised an eyebrow, expecting more. "It's a thing," I started. "Maybe we could talk later, after work?"

"Sure."

There was that damn word again, the one filled with so many questions.

I gripped the bull by the horns. "Or now? When we park, I need to tell you something about a recording." He glanced at me, curious, and then, eyes back on the road as we rounded the final corner. "It wasn't me—"

"Shit! No!"

We jerked to a stop, and I tensed at the emotion in Bryce's tone as he scrambled out of the car.

But all I could see were paramedics, cop cars, and flashing blue lights past a cordon.

And beyond it, a crowd, hiding the garden entrance from our sight.

Chapter 18

Bryce

I WAS SURE I WAS ABOUT TO BE ARRESTED FOR SHOVING a cop.

Only he gave me a shove in return that nearly knocked me off my feet. If not for Michael catching me, I'd have been sprawled in the gutter.

"Listen buddy…" the cop began.

"This is my garden. What's going on? Where is my son?" I moved around the cop at the gate with attitude, stepping into the community garden, ignoring the whispers and attempted pats from my unsheltered friends lingering outside the fence. "Leo?!" I bellowed as I raced inside, skidding to a halt. The garden was in chaos. Pots thrown about, plants broken, the greenhouse door hanging on one hinge, and my office window busted. Frantic didn't even begin to cover how I was feeling.

"Dad!" Leo shouted, breaking away from a female

police officer to dart toward me. I broke into a dead run, catching him in midair. Mrs. Cho was deep in conversation with an older cop who looked a great deal like Sly Stallone in his *Expendables* days.

"Leo, Leo," I whispered, kissing his messy hair as I held him close.

"Dad, you're squishing me," Leo whined so I loosened my hold. Just a bit. I might never let go of him ever again. Didn't matter how old he got.

"Sorry, sorry, I saw the cops and…" Panicked didn't sound like something a composed parent should be. "Worried. I was worried. What happened here?"

Now that I knew Leo and Mrs. Cho were safe, I could draw a semi-normal breath.

"It was *awesome!*" He wiggled free, his body humming with excitement that one usually saw after he downed a Mountain Dew Code Red. "We got up and had breakfast! And then, we walked here to do tai chi because Mrs. Cho said it's a stepping stone to karate." I wasn't sure if that was true or not. Perhaps the boy made it up. "So, we came here to do moves, then this ginormous dude with tattoos showed up. He started throwing things around and tore out a whole bunch of Mrs. Lee's corn plants, then he tried to grab me and… and… Mrs. Cho kicked him in the kneecap! Like *Hi-Ya!*" He did a roundhouse kick that nearly took out a green pepper plant. "And then… and then she… and then she smashed him in the face with a clay pot full of oregano! Ker-Smash! Holy chitters, Dad, it was just like

Fist of the Golden Monkey! He called her a really bad name that rhymes with stitch, then limped off after throwing a pot of mint through your window as a warning about five hundred a day. Dad, she was amazing! Can I take karate lessons *and* hockey lessons?!"

Michael made a sound behind me as if he were being sick. I glanced back to see that yes, he was pale, but no, he was not vomiting. I might though. What the hell was all this about? Five hundred what? Pickled peppers? Did the man think we had big money lying around here? Local thugs knew this place was a wasteland in terms of things to steal. They'd hit us up numerous times until they finally realized that shovels and hand trowels didn't net much on the black market. We'd not been vandalized or broken into for over a year.

"We'll talk about karate later. I need to speak to Mrs. Cho and the police. Are you sure you're okay?"

"Yeah, I ran and hid behind the compost bins. My hands are poopy, see?" He showed me grimy hands and nails. "I made a bunch of poop and rotten veggie balls to throw at the tattoo man in case he came for me, but Mrs. Cho took care of him good! She's a national hero!"

"That she is," I coughed out, taking my boy by the hand, and leading him to the cop who was writing down Mrs. Cho's statement. Michael went into the greenhouse, to tidy things up I assumed, maybe right the door. Shaking from the shock of it all, I nonetheless listened to Mrs. Cho describing what had happened, my grip on my son tight. No way was he leaving my side until his wedding day, and his spouse had best be trained in military hand-to-hand combat tactics before I handed him over.

Ten or fifteen minutes passed. The cops on the beat were not overly concerned about the vandalism. They told us they would investigate, possibly have Mrs. Cho come to the precinct to examine some mug shots, and then, that would probably be it.

"Not to be a jerk here, but this kind of shit happens all the time in this neighborhood," Officer Hank Perth told us around a stick of gum wadded into his right cheek. "Vandals always looking for shit to steal. Probably, it was one of those bums outside your property—"

"We prefer the term unsheltered person," I pointed out, Leo slumped at my side, bored of talking to the cops.

"Right, well, it was probably some unsheltered person new to the streets that thought you folks had some cash lying around. Sorry about the destruction. Call your insurance agent. And if you have any more trouble call."

Off they went, the unsheltered folk at the gate scattering like frightened doves when a cat showed up in the park. They'd all had run-ins with the local constabulary.

I glanced down at Mrs. Cho as she rattled off something in Korean.

"English please?"

"I said they are useless as tits on bull."

I had to smirk. Then, I had to hug her. "Thank you for defending my son." She patted my back as I took a small moment to break into a tiny little moment. Nothing huge, just several deep shaky breaths now that the danger was past. "I'm so happy that you both are safe."

"Ah, that ape face never stood a chance." She broke free, wiped down her baggy pants and shirt, then looked around. She never was one for big emotional scenes. "I wanted to kick his balls into his sinus, but he was too tall, so I go for vulnerable spot number two."

"Right, yes, well thank you for keeping Leo safe." I finally let go of my son's hand. He bolted into the greenhouse to regale Michael of the super cool moment. I blew out a long, slow breath as the thought of relaying this incident to Courtney reared its ugly head. "Shit, I have to tell his mother about this."

"No law says you have to tell her," she offered.

"The parent law says that I do. Shit, she is going to come unglued."

"Meh, she might be okay."

Courtney was *not* okay.

She was about as far from okay as a woman could

get. Like if okay was Earth, she was in a nebula where only the *USS Enterprise* had ventured.

It was two hours past the shake-up at the community gardens. The vandalism had been fixed for the most part. A new door for the greenhouse was being delivered tomorrow from a local home and garden center,—free of charge—and installed. The plants that had been disturbed had been replanted, and my office window had some plywood over it until we could afford a new window. I did want to make a run to the nearby hardware store to buy some security lights. Michael had said he would call in a favor, lean on his former celebrity life and get them. I didn't question him, but it would be great if we could rig them up before sundown.

Leo, Michael, and I were back at my place, pizza lunch eaten, as Leo was gathering his clothes up for the trip home. It was two days sooner than planned, but given the state my ex was in, I didn't argue when she said he was coming home *now.* Like right now, Bryce, you miserable loser asshole. She didn't say the bad stuff, I added that for flavor, but she had demanded her baby come home. Now.

"… told you a thousand times that your neighborhood is dangerous. Surely you make enough money to find a better place away from all the gangs and drug lords and hookers!"

I sighed into the phone as she railed away. Michael sat on the sofa, his latest slice of pizza untouched on his plate, staring at a thundercloud Storm plushie he'd given Leo a few days ago.

"There are no hookers," I managed to wiggle into the tirade. Court wasn't listening. When she ran out of steam, we ended the call. I flopped down beside Michael, head throbbing, as my son could be heard making Jean-Claude Van Damme martial arts shouts in my bedroom. Good thing Mrs. Cho liked the kid. "So that was pleasant."

"I'm so sorry," Michael whispered.

I patted his thick thigh. "No need to apologize. You didn't do anything. Tony found a flight out of LAX leaving in two hours. I'm going to fly him home, then come back. I should be home by midnight if there are no delays. Do you still want to grab those motion lights for the garden or wait until tomorrow?"

His sad gaze lifted from the plushie to me. "I'll get them and see if I can hook them up. Then we need to talk."

I stared at him with concern. Was he dumping me after one magical night over some mishap at the garden? Surely, one case of vandalism wasn't cause enough for—

"It's not about us. I mean… I'm not breaking this thing with us off, but you might want to."

I gaped, opened my mouth to speak, and was interrupted by my son, bags packed, darting in to grab Stormy the Storm mascot.

"Okay, I'm ready," Leo announced, eyes bright. He

loved flying. The flight attendants always fussed over him, patting his head, and slipping him extra packets of nuts or cans of soda. "Are you going to come see me play hockey in two weeks?" Leo asked as I rose, my sight still on my lover, to leave.

"Wouldn't miss it. Michael?" I prodded and got a nod from the woe-is-me man on my sofa. "Great. We'll plan a two-day trip then. We better go buddy."

Leo hugged Michael tight, smiled at him, then ran to the front door.

"I'll meet you at the garden?" I asked as I slipped my feet into my old sandals.

"Yeah, we'll talk there." Michael got up, left his uneaten food on the coffee table, and with a ruffle of Leo's hair, left. Right. That wasn't ominous or anything.

"Dad, come on, I don't want to miss the plane."

"Sorry, just lost in outer space, bud."

Six grueling hours later, I was back in LA, my ass sore for a variety of reasons—the wild sex with Michael last night and the stellar ass-chewing from my ex at the airport when I'd taken him back. She'd blasted me in the face with my ineptitude as a father, right at the Delta departure check-in desk. People lining up had gotten an earful. I was just glad that Tony had taken Leo to the nearest sweet shop to peruse the candies while I was ripped a new one. Now, I was back in LA, worn-out mentally and physically, and about to face whatever it was that Michael was carrying inside him.

When the taxi dropped me off, I was pleased to see the garden office was lit up. Using my key, I let myself inside, finding Michael tinkering with something in the fuse box.

"Hey," I called to not startle him. He jumped anyway. Understandable, given what had taken place here this morning. "Sorry. I didn't mean to scare you. The lights look good."

"Yeah, they're nice, but they keep kicking the breaker when they come on. We might need to get an electrician out here for this." He closed the fuse box, faced me, then motioned to my wobbly office chair. "You should sit down."

"Michael, I know that you're probably spooked over what took place here, but trust me, a rogue vandal in this neighborhood isn't something new."

"It's not…" He pulled a hand over his face, his eyes hollow. "Just sit please."

So, I sat. Even though I had been sitting for hours on seats that were too hard, too narrow, and too close to the airplane bathrooms. Even though my ass longed for some soothing cream. I sat, and I waited. He paced, working his hands into fists, then shaking them out.

"Okay, so there's this guy called Looper," he began, his shoulders tight and high as if he expected a punch to the gut.

I nodded, saying nothing, allowing him to speak as we did in group, uninterrupted. He gave me a sorrowful look, then dove into his tale. The longer he spoke, the more shocked I was. Gangsters, racketeering, blackmail, illegal sports betting, and Michael somehow caught up in the middle of it all. When he finished, he stalled out by the far wall, leaning against the wall-mounted unit of shelves filled with gardening supplies.

"That's… that's some story," I managed to force out. "And this Looper. He has a recording of you saying you'd throw a game, and he's the one who sent his goon to come here and threaten my son and landlord?"

"Yeah, I think so. The threats are the same. Fuck, I'm sorry for dragging you and Leo into this shitty mess of mine."

He slid to the floor, his face in his hands, strong shoulders quaking as he began to weep silently. I moved to his side as fast as my cramped, tired old body could, dropping to the cool cement floor to place my arm around his neck. He tried to turn away, but I led his face to my shoulder, tucking his damp cheek against my throat.

"We'll sort this all out, don't worry." I kissed his hair just as I had Leo's several hours ago. Had it only been twelve or so hours? It felt like an eternity. How did the most wonderful night, then morning, of my life veer into this dark place? I suppose what they say is true.

For every joy, a soul must know a sorrow. "I know someone we can call."

"If they'd hurt Leo, I would have…" He choked up, unable to finish that thought. I cringed at the mention of my boy being harmed, but kept it locked down. I'd rehash all of this in group someday. Right now, Michael needed me. And he needed help. As much as I dreaded making the call.

"Leo is fine. It was a big lark to him, a kung-fu flick come to life with Mrs. Cho as the star. He's blissfully unaware of the reasons, and we're going to make sure it stays that way. But for now, you need to get out from under this hood and his henchman. I'm going to call Jack."

"Who?" He swiped at his eyes with his fingertips as if the tears burned. I had to reckon hockey players didn't cry often. Seeing his tears felt as though it was a good thing. Cathartic maybe. Lord knows I'd wept an ocean of tears in my time. But a sobbing gardener was more acceptable than a weepy winger. Toxic masculinity sucks.

"My brother-in-law. Ex brother-in-law." I tensed as we discussed Jackson.

"Oh, the dickhead."

"Yep, the dickhead. He's part of some special division of the LAPD that deals with organized crime."

"No shit," he whispered, pulling himself together as best he could. I nodded, pecked his damp cheek, and snuggled in close. "I've tried to not bring the cops into this. Looper said he would put an end to my skating."

"I think this is well past what you can handle yourself. What if they go after Charles and his family next?" Michael's face fell. "Can I call Jack?"

"God, what a fucking mess I've made of everything. Why the hell do you even love me?"

I took his face between my hands. "I love you because you fuck up. We all fuck up, Michael. You've just found yourself in a spot that requires a helping hand. Let me be that hand."

He stared into my eyes as if he could find an answer there. I hoped he found more than an answer. I hoped he found all the love and faith I had in him.

"Okay yeah, call the cop."

I pecked the tip of his nose, dug out my cell, and made the call. I'd have sooner had a tooth extracted with no Novocain than dial Jack's number.

"Jackson Winwood, speak," Jack said into my ear, his voice still that smoky rasp I knew and loathed.

"Jack, it's Bryce."

"Jesus loving Christ," he sighed. It was his favorite saying.

"He has nothing to do with my call."

"Bryce, I'm tired. It's midnight. My alarm will go off in four hours. Also, I really don't like you all that much, so I'm going to hang up now and pretend this was a bad dream from the cold Mexican food I had on stakeout tonight. Good—"

"There's this guy called Looper who's been harassing my boyfriend and threatening him …." I blurted out everything that Michael had told me before Jack could hang up.

There was a long-ass pause. I heard Jack's bedding rustling, then the flick of a lighter followed by a long, weary inhalation of a Newport menthol cigarette—if he still smoked that brand.

"Your boyfriend?"

"Out of all that, you're picking up that item?"

"Just didn't know you played for both teams. That makes you only slightly less of a jerk."

"Gee, thanks." Jack had come out as gay several years ago, daring the men in his division to say one word other than 'congrats Jack.' Very few people pushed Jackson around. "So can you come to the San Pedro Community Garden?"

Another exhale. Bryce was wringing his hands beside me. "I'll come, but only because this scummy sewer rat thought he could threaten my nephew. Sit tight. And tell your boyfriend that he's got terrible taste in men."

"The gate code is 6722," I said, then worried I shouldn't be handing that out. The gate was a deterrent to vandals, in as much as anyone could climb the walls because of the amount of low hanging tree branches. Still, Jackson *was* a cop. An asshole, but also a cop.

"Got it."

The call ended. I sighed. Then, Michael and I sat on

the floor side-by-side, whispering until someone rapped on the door. We both jumped.

"Who is it?" I called, glancing around for a weapon. Nothing was close at hand other than a six-pack of cello seedling packets. Not exactly a lethal weapon.

"Detective Jackson Winwood, LAPD Organized Crimes Division. You want to see my fucking badge, Bryce?"

Okay, yeah, that was Jackson. Gravel-throated and ill-tempered as ever.

I really did want to make him show us the ID, but knowing how grumpy Jack was even when it wasn't almost one in the morning, I gave Michael a nod, rose, and went to the office door and opened it. There, on the other side, stood six-foot-five inches of burly, golden-haired, green-eyed cop reeking of exhaustion, coffee, and cigarette smoke.

"You look just as pissy as ever," I said in lieu of a proper greeting.

"It's the look I strive for," he said as he stepped inside. His eyes fell on Michael, and his mouth fell open. Okay, that was a good look. It didn't happen often. "Storm. Suspended. Criminal Record. Gambling," he summarized in bullet points. "This should be interesting." Then, he rolled his eyes. "Why don't we make some coffee and have us a sit-down, Zeetoo?"

Chapter 19

Michael

THERE WAS NO LOVE LOST BETWEEN JACKSON AND Bryce, and I found myself cautious, wondering what his appearance meant.

Jackson glanced at his phone, a frown creasing his forehead. "Why is my sister calling in the middle of the night?" he muttered, more to himself than to us. He answered the call, his expression growing tighter with every passing second. I noticed he kept his eyes locked on Bryce, a hard, assessing stare that didn't waver. The tension in his body language spoke volumes, and I couldn't help but wonder what was being said on the other end of the line.

"I'll talk to him," he said, and his tone was even, but the spark of temper in his eyes was terrifying. He placed his cell on the table, and for a moment, I didn't know what was happening, and then, in a flurry of movement he was up and dragging Bryce to the wall. "Is Looper your supplier?"

"What? No!"

"I thought you were over that shit!" he yelled in Bryce's face.

I was up and out of my chair so fast it toppled over. I yanked at Jackson's arm, but he was this huge immoveable object, so I shimmied under and up between Jackson and Bryce and used my bodyweight to lever him off.

"Fuck off!" I shouted.

For a second, Jackson backed down, and then, just as I relaxed, he was back at trying to grip Bryce, but I stood steady and stopped him, shoving him away.

"You told me you were done!" Jackson accused Bryce. "Then I find out you've put Leo in danger?"

"Bryce didn't!" I snapped and shoved Jackson back again. He stood his ground, I stood mine, and we were two warriors on edge and waiting to battle. Adrenaline flowed, and I tensed, only relaxing when Bryce put a hand on my shoulder.

"It's okay," he said gently. "I've got this."

I didn't move though, so Bryce had to talk around me, as Jackson and I stared at each other.

"I've been clean for nearly five years, Jackson, and I would never put my son in any danger."

Jackson was incredulous and shook his head. "Leo was here, and you had a fucking drug dealer on your premises."

"No, he didn't," I said.

But Jackson wasn't listening. "He's done it before—got so high my sister and Leo were in danger."

"He's right," Bryce said in a small voice that broke my heart.

I shoved at Jackson again. "Sit down," I snapped, and then, turned my back to him, seeing Bryce against the wall, one hand pressed to his heart and his eyes bright with emotion. "Bryce?"

"I never told you, how low I went... how nothing mattered except for the pills... how not even my baby boy..." His eyes swam with tears, and I cradled his face, wiped a loose tear on his cheek with my thumb.

"It's okay," I murmured. "We all fuck up, you said that to me, right? You've made your peace, you're a good person, Leo loves you, and his mom doesn't hate you."

"But—"

"I love you, Bryce. You have me, okay? You have this garden and all the good you do, and the people who love you."

He nodded, and I pressed a kiss to his lips.

"I should have told you all of this. It changes how you feel—"

I stopped him with another kiss. "No. Whatever we've done, however our addictions have hurt us and others, I will never change how I feel."

He slumped a little, and I think it might have been relief. "I love you," he murmured.

"I love you."

Behind us, Jackson cleared his throat. "As touching as this is, you wanna tell me why Looper is up in your business, Bryce?"

I searched Bryce's expression, and willed him to be strong, for himself, and selfishly for me.

"I'm here for you," he whispered.

"And I'm here for you," I returned, and we had one last kiss, until Jackson clearing his throat stopped us. I took Bryce's hand, or did he take mine? Either way, our fingers were laced as we sat at the table opposite a grumpy-ass detective. I extended my other hand to shake, which Jackson took.

"Michael Zhang," I said.

"I know who you are, Zeetoo," he replied.

I smiled at him then, somehow the nickname didn't seem as offensive as I remembered. From his lips, it didn't sound like an insult, more that he knew our team, maybe he was a fan, maybe knew hockey, and hell, it had been a long journey, but I was proud of being the second Zhang, when the first Zhang was as freaking amazing as my older brother.

"Call me Michael," I murmured, and he inclined his head.

"Call me Jack," he answered, and shot a glance at Bryce who was very quiet. "Sorry," he said to his ex-brother-in-law. "It's been a shit day, and it's no excuse, but I'm so fucking tired."

Bryce smiled then. "It's all good."

"No, you don't deserve my shit," Jack added, then sighed, rubbing at his temples. "So, does someone want to tell me about why the name Looper is connected to anything at all?"

So, I did.

And it was painful, and cathartic, and humbling.

But I told him everything, and his exhaustion fled as he made notes, and by the time we were done, it was nearly dawn, and all three of us were exhausted. I watched Jack bro-hug Bryce, murmuring something as he left, and then, it was just the two of us as I shut the door. I hated to think that Jack had dripped poison in Bryce's ears, because after all the bluster, Jack seemed like a good guy.

But Bryce was my guy, and I would always have his back.

"What did he say?" I asked with caution.

Bryce shook his head in disbelief, and then, smiled, and the smile reached his eyes. "He said I was a good dad. That Leo couldn't have a better father."

I kissed his smile.

Yeah, Jack was one of the good guys.

"I'm not sure about this," Bryce murmured, tugging me to a stop right outside the back entrance to the Storm training facility. That should've been my line because I was sure as shit not happy about attending this thing, but Charles had begged, Hope and Grace had begged, and so here I was, attending a family skate on fresh-laid ice, my skates in my duffle and a new pair for Bryce right alongside them. It wouldn't be the entire team here, but enough of them that I was nervous.

Only Bryce wasn't worried about any of that because he'd never skated in his entire life.

"Daaaadd," Leo whined and danced around us, his own Storm duffle over his shoulder, wearing a Storm jersey with Charles's number on the back. He'd wanted to wear mine, but it hadn't seemed right, because I wasn't sure I was coming back in any capacity. The negotiation for my return, after metrics showed I could be an asset, had floundered, and two weeks out from the vandalism at the garden—working with Jack, and loving Bryce every minute I could—I didn't need hockey.

Didn't want it.

Go figure.

At least not the competitive side of it—but getting back on the ice and feeling the freedom, yeah, I wanted that.

Bryce ruffled Leo's hair, then, shoulders back, he continued the walk, but he did side-eye me with an added frown.

"I won't let you fall on your ass," I reassured him.

"Pfft."

I patted said ass. "I like it too much."

That got a smile, and we finally reached the door, Charles waiting on the other side to let us in. He separated me from Bryce and Leo and gestured through to the ice. "You have five Mikey, all on your own before anyone gets here."

I kissed Bryce, nodded at Charles, fist-bumped Leo, then near-sprinted down the short corridor and to the locker room, discarding my shoes and strapping on my skates at the speed of light.

Charles opened the door, tossed something at me that I caught out of instinct—a hockey stick—and then he grinned. "Go get 'em."

Walking back into the rink after all this time felt surreal. The familiar chill of the ice hit me first, then a wave of nostalgia and adrenaline. I stepped out and as I took those first few glides, the feel of the cold stuff under my skates, the sense of freedom and control, it all came rushing back. I felt at home again, despite the time away. I built up speed in the corners, completed a couple of circuits, zoomed in and around the net, recalled all the training sessions, loved every second of it, but when I caught sight of Bryce leaning over the boards, I iced to a stop right in front of him.

He was grinning hard.

"I've never seen you so sexy," he murmured.

I paused a minute for a kiss. "Not even when I'm weeding?"

He took a moment to fake-consider. "Well, your ass in the air is a very good thing."

"Come on," I held out a hand, and guided him to the break in the barrier, opening the gate and waiting for him to take a step onto the ice. He was already wobbly as shit on dry land, but we took off the blade protectors, and then, my man placed one blade on the ice and his eyes widened.

"Don't let me fall," he muttered.

"Too late, because you fell for me," I teased.

He smiled, and before he knew it, he was six feet from the wall, gliding with me as I skated backward. I kissed him, in the middle of the rink, and began to move, holding him close, keeping him steady, as we were cruising the oval, then I switched so I was at his side and not in front of him. He wobbled a little at the realization of where he was and what he was doing, but I tightened my grip and gave him something to lean on.

Just like I wanted to do for the rest of his life.

The same as he let me lean on him.

The shadow of what Jack had asked me to do with Looper was hanging around, but today, I didn't want it anywhere near us—that was for another day.

For now, Bryce was in a world so familiar to me, and I felt a sense of responsibility, wanting to make this experience enjoyable and safe for him. His trust in me, his willingness to step into my world, was so amazing, and as we skated in slow circuits of the ice, his tentative steps becoming more confident, I realized how much I loved sharing this part of my life with him.

He whooped as we passed behind the net, raising his other hand in joy.

"Do you want me to let go?" I asked, and boy did that raised hand drop fast as he glanced at me.

"Fuck no!" he said, but he was laughing.

And it was everything.

The sound of voices, of clattering, of Leo chattering with Charles, all kinds of excited, pulled us out of the loops and the swirls and the joy of the ice, and my heart froze.

There were people here that I'd shut out.

People who could hate me for what I'd done to the Storm.

And fuck me if the first person I saw wasn't Coach Hudain, frowning at me and gesturing for me to come his way. I guided us back to the barrier and helped Bryce to steady.

"I just need a moment. Will you be okay?" I murmured.

He nodded, although his grip on the barrier was white-knuckled until Charles skated over and took my place.

I headed to Coach, who'd placed himself way down the rink, away from the arriving team and their families, and iced to a stop—sue me if he hated the showboating.

"Zeetoo," he said and nodded.

"Coach," I responded in kind, and didn't even correct him to call me Michael. He'd never called me anything but my nickname or my number, and it all felt familiar. I was still harboring the anger at what he'd said to me on the phone, saying he didn't want me, letting me hear that. The things I *needed* to hear.

"Look here, Zeetoo—"

"No, please," in for a penny, in for a pound. "I don't need any more speeches about how I let people down. I know you thought that—"

"Are you disrespecting me?" Coach interjected.

I blinked. "No—"

"Then listen to your coach," he demanded.

And somehow, I slipped back into being the winger on a team I was no longer part of. "But—"

"Are you listening?"

I glanced over to where Bryce was still gripping the side of the rink. For him, and for us, I could put up with another lecture. If only to keep the peace. "Yes, Coach."

He sighed then. "Look, Michael, I owe you an apology. I was wrong to go off on you about the team. The pressure they put on the coaching team when it comes to money, forcing us to… look… I saw you were struggling because I know the way you play, and you weren't yourself, and all I did was turn a blind eye."

What? Was this an apology? Or some reverse psychology? Or pity.

"I don't need pity—"

"When you reached the bottom, I wasn't there to

help you up. I should have been, and I'm sorry." He extended a hand for me to shake.

"I'm not coming back, even if they want me," I said cautiously, wondering if the hand would drop.

It didn't.

So, after a pause, we shook hands.

"If you want my opinion," Coach said, "You're making the right choice for you. Fuck the money."

I snorted a laugh. "Yeah, fuck the money."

Chapter 20

Bryce

It was amazing how much fun I could have at a skating party when I wasn't skating.

I'd gone to my ass several times, each fall hurting more than the previous one, before opting to de-skate and chill on the sidelines with the players' families. Leo had taken to the ice like a duck to water. Obviously, a trait he'd gotten from his mother because my skating skills were dismal. Courtney had come around after speaking to her brother in depth the other day. Which was the single reason that Leo was here. I didn't really want to owe Jackson anything, our relationship was still rocky, but he *had* gotten his sister to see that I wasn't the bad guy, nor was Michael. The bad guys were this Marco "Looper" Marchetti and his ilk.

"Hey, are you done skating?" Michael asked, sliding up to the glass where I was seated with several lovely ladies discussing gardening. I held up my foot to show him my sandaled toes. Toes that were quite chilly. "Ah man, that's a bummer."

"My backside disagrees," I said, then smiled at a man carrying a dish heaped with food, who dropped down beside me. My brain stuttered as I drank in the handsome face of Finn Kerrigan. Movie star.

"Hey Michael! Did you try the chicken fingers? They're delicious. Hello Bryce! I'd shake, but my hands are full." He tried to wiggle his left hand, but the mountain of grub balanced on his plate negated that movement. "We could noggin knock in greeting!"

So, we bumped foreheads. Michael grinned, gave me a soft kiss, then returned to the ice to guide Leo around. Seeing them together made me warm inside.

"So, you and Michael. That's nice. He's a good guy who just found himself in a bit of a mess," Finn said around a fat tender dripping mustard sauce onto a serving of curly fries. "Cam likes him and his brother a lot. I do too. Did you meet him at rehab?"

I blinked.

He blushed. "Sorry, I'm so sorry. Sometimes, I just say things. Forget that I asked that."

"It's fine." I picked up a crisp stalk of celery from my rather meager plate. It was hard to avoid meat at times, especially at catered events geared for family fun. Kids did love their chicken nuggets and fish sticks. "We met at the community garden."

"Oh right. I really loved that place. Everyone raved about the platters you provided for our wedding."

"I'm glad they were so popular." I thought back to that day. When I was delivering the food, that was the first time I had seen Michael. He'd been drunk, angry, and obnoxious. The rage had rolled off the man. Though I'd learned now, that amid the ire was so much hurt and fear. Things he was still working though. Recovery was an ongoing process, every day we faced temptations.

"Mm, so tasty and fresh. How goes things at the garden?"

"Oh, well, it's fine." I paused to chew a bite of celery.

"Cool. And the people who you help out with free veggies?"

I glanced to the side. Finn was munching away, but I could feel the weight of his gaze on me, and I took a chance.

"To be honest, they could use some help. As you know, the unsheltered in this city aren't treated with all that much respect. They're run off like unwanted vermin when most are in need of what we should be offering to all our citizens. Things like mental health services, addiction therapy, and affordable housing. Last count had forty-six thousand homeless, and most of them are veterans or families. The city has closed down camps and moved some into hotels, but few of the unsheltered are in permanent homes. Funding for the program will run out eventually, and those people will be back on the streets. There has to be a way to fund affordable housing to those who need it the most." Everything spilled out in one go, and Finn's eyes were wide.

"Wow," Finn whispered, laying his half eaten tender back to his plate.

Kids and hockey players skated past, smiles, and laughs everywhere, and here I stood on my soap box.

"I'm sorry. It's just something that I see every day. I shouldn't bring my personal worries into a team family event."

"No, hey, no. I love your passion, and the fact that you care. What do you think we can do to help the unsheltered?"

We? "Do you mean you'd like to help?" Getting a huge star like Finn Kerrigan behind any kind of initiative would be incredible.

"Sure, and I know Cam would too. The whole team probably. Hold this." He shoved his food at me, shot to his feet, and raced off. Michael and Leo, accompanied by Charles and his girls, skated past, Leo's eyes flaring when he spied the meat-filled platter in my left hand. I'd have some explaining to do it seemed. One of the skaters out there was twirling about like a figure skater, toes pointed, arms extended, only to be knocked over by one of the others, who then teased him unmercifully. I waited for it to come to blows, but the two of them fell to the floor laughing.

Finn returned in what seemed like two seconds with an older bald man in a Storm jersey, along with Clare Zhang and four other women.

"This is Hal." I shook hands with Hal, he of the bald pate and oversized Chavkin jersey.

"You know Clare, obviously, and this is Amanda, Penelope, and Christine." More shaking. "They're part of the Players' Spouses of the Storm Program or PSSP, like you're calling a cat." Everyone chuckled. "They're all ears to talk about how the team, and the spouses of the players—and yes us hubbies and boyfriends are included—can aid in your new initiative. So, the floor is yours!"

I fumbled and bumbled, tripping over my own tongue, but then found enough presence of mind to explain what I was hoping to achieve to the small, but eager group. We chatted for over forty minutes, and the talk ended when a short silence fell over the rink as a new person stepped out onto the ice, a huge man with two small girls, one on either side of him.

"Greetings from New York," the mountain of muscle said, his sharp gaze fixed on the rest of the team. "You got some funny trees out here," he tacked on, pulling a laugh from the guys. Everyone skated over to him, friendly ribbing and handshaking taking place as his daughters, I assumed, clung to his thick thighs.

"That's Oliver Cowen," Clare filled me in, then took a sip from her tiny bottle of grapefruit juice and lowered her voice. "They call him Cowboy, and he's just signed with the Storm. He played for over sixteen years in New York. Widowed two years ago. Took the trade so he could live closer to his mother and father out in Carmel. They're retired from some sort of foreign service for the government. Diplomats, I think, but I could be wrong on that. Anyway, they're going to help with the girls when he plays. His wife died of breast cancer, and he took a year off from hockey to mourn and be with his daughters. Seems like a committed dad and was super popular in New York where he played a gritty and reliable defensive slot." She sat back and sipped more grapefruit juice.

I gaped at Clare. "You're like a walking Storm players encyclopedia."

She did a perfect Alexis Rose from *Schitt's Creek* happy little hair flip. "Thanks. It's a gift."

"So, who's the one who can do all the twirling skating?"

She frowned, then it cleared. "Oh, that's Craig Beaulieu, he's so sweet, did some figure skating as a kid, almost went professional, but decided hockey was more his thing."

"Craig, okay." I thought he looked very graceful out there, despite the stick he was wielding.

We watched Oliver— *Cowboy*—glide around the ice on his skates, his girls staying close, but then Leo was chatting to them, and they joined the kids' group. My son was such a good kid, even though I was biased and didn't care who knew it. There was talking on the ice, then the men out there skating broke into small squads, some pulling on white jerseys, some blue, all leaving the distinctive purple jerseys with their significant others.

And sue me if I thought Michael looked damn sexy in his white top and hugged the M. Zhang jersey he'd tossed to me way too tight.

And yes, I might have sniffed it as well, but no one would have seen that.

"Oh, this is fun. A little three on three," Clare said as I nibbled on some rather corky carrots. Whoever the caterer bought their produce from was lacking. "They usually do this to raise money for local charities, but this seems to just be for fun. How about we girls—and guys—add something more to the game. Let's say for every goal our hubbies score we donate a thousand dollars to the soon-to-be LA Storm Affordable Housing Foundation."

"Now Clare…" Hal warned, but the players' wives, and husband in the shape of Finn, were already sold on the idea of helping the unsheltered. All I could think was thank goodness I wasn't included because a thousand dollars was out of my league. I did wonder if they should be using money on something Michael was part of—these casual dollar challenges on things were likely endemic—but it wasn't harming anyone. Right?

I glanced at the small group—were any of them on the edge of an addiction?

If they were, then who was I to comment?

She smiled, waved him off, and nudged me in the side. I liked Clare. I suspected that once she set her mind to something, it got done, which was what the people suffering out on the streets needed.

It took a few moments for the goalies to get geared up, but once they were in net, the play started. Leo and Clare's girls, as well as the two Cowen children, flopped down around us, skates gone, sneakers on feet, and plates filled with kid fare. I gave Leo a hair ruffle that did nothing to slow his ingestion of breaded chicken strips dripping with honey.

The skating started off slow, the Storm guys moving up and down the ice, passing the puck as they teased each other. Coach sat a few rows behind us, watching, sipping on something hot, his eyes on the team as they messed around. Perhaps, it was just a fun exercise for the players, but for the head coach, who had been under fire from the fans for a mediocre performance this season, it was something more. Maybe, it was a chance for him to see how the new man, Cowboy, and the returning man—if Michael did return to the ice—might fit into the roster.

He hadn't said anything to me about whether he was returning, but the way he spoke about his recovery hinted that maybe he wouldn't be back. I glanced up at the coach, who nodded at me, then smiled, and I faced the ice.

My boyfriend was smooth as silk, gliding around,

shifting the puck to others wearing the same color, when Oliver shunted Michael away from the puck with a shoulder nudge. The men in white hooted at the steal and the soft shot on goal, and then, things got a little more serious. Nothing too harsh, no strong checks, but I could see the competitiveness in all the players coming to the fore. Michael had words with Oliver that made the big D-man laugh.

I did take note that Oliver would check his watch after every shift.

They played on for about thirty minutes, five goals scored total, before the spontaneous game was called due to someone's kid having to be at a soccer practice at six. Maybe it was Oliver's daughter who had to go, and that was why he was so intent on his wristwatch. Clare and I herded our three wild ones and met Michael and Charles outside the Storm dressing room.

"We're going to watch movies when we get home," Clare announced when we were loading kids and hockey gear into our cars. Michael had yet to get his license back, something that gnawed at him, but I was happy to take us where we needed to go in my old beater. "Why don't you send Leo over to the house, and you two can have some couple time?"

"No, I couldn't ask you to do that," I said.

She gave me that look. I laughed. Leo also threw me a pleading stare. I was nervous about letting Leo out of my sight given what had taken place with Mrs. Cho. Looper and his goons were still moving through the shadows of the City of Angels, which made me more than nervous. Whatever Jack was doing about all of that, he was taking his sweet old time.

"You didn't ask. I offered. And he'll be just a pool's distance away. We have state-of-the-art security. I promise you; he'll be safe."

"Okay, yes, of course he will. Thank you." I took her hand between mine, then squeezed. Leo did need to spend time with children, even though I wanted to be with him twenty-four-seven. "When he's ready to come to the pool house, just text Michael, and we'll walk over to get him."

"We can do that." Clare smiled with understanding, knowing that parents worried all the time. It was part of the job, a part I'd been told would never end. Leo was thrilled, and as soon as we were parked in Charles's sweeping drive, he and the girls ran inside, leaving us behind like unwanted shoes.

Charles gave Michael a soft shove toward the pool house. I followed, sliding my hand into his, the warm breeze ruffling the fronds on the palms as we made our way into the small, but now familiar, home.

With a click of the front door, we headed towards each other, all strong arms, soft lips, and gentle caresses. Getting naked, we tumbled into his bed and lost ourselves to the passion that always flared like a wildfire at a mere touch. Michael lay on his left side, me on my right, and we kissed for ages. His large hand wrapped around our cocks, the satiny glide unravelling the tight hold I'd had on myself since that morning at the garden. I let myself flow on the sensations like a man on a raft with no rudder. I let his kisses and strokes carry me along, the ebb and flow of passion a gentle current. With his lips on mine, I came with a soft whimper, his climax coming a moment or two after mine.

Afterwards, we took a long shower, slotting together as best we could in the tiny space under the warm water, his fingers massaging shampoo into my hair as I worked a soapy lather up on his hairy chest.

We headed back to his bed, sated, in our briefs, the sheet pulled up as the ceiling fan whirred overhead.

"So, I talked to Coach," he began with caution. "I've made a decision."

"Okay?" I didn't know what I wanted for him right then. If I was going to be selfish, I worried that going back to hockey would be too much for him, that he'd lose his way, but it wasn't my choice.

Together, we'd weather any storm.

"I told him I'm not going back to hockey, not to the Storm, even if they wanted me, or any other team,." he paused, and I laced our fingers and squeezed. "I want to maybe coach, like with the veterans' team, something that isn't so…" he huffed, and I filled in the rest myself. Something not so life-stealing as a full-time professional career. "Anyway, I don't know what else I'll do. I mean, I have some ideas, but for now, I'm done."

"Okay."

"Does that sound right to you?"

He sounded so nervous, as if I were going to disagree with him, but my heart was settled with him making this decision.

"I think it's a good decision."

"I think so too. Thought maybe I could visit the gardens, work with you, sometimes, if you want me."

"I'll always want you." We lay in silence for a moment. "I never thought anything could soothe my soul like the dunes, but lying here in your arms feels just as serene," I whispered as the sounds of night flitted in through the window.

"I'm glad."

I moved and nestled into his side; my head pillowed on his arm. I admired his profile in the dim light of the moon. "I could write a song about the way Luna paints your face."

"Ooh, poetic," he teased.

I reached up to trace the upturned corner of his mouth. "I used to be. Now? I'm not sure. Most of the things that I write, I trash. I feel like the muses have left me, drowned out by narcotics filling my brain."

"I'm sorry that happened to you."

I ran the pad of my index finger along his nose, my mind light and airy, floating to times past. "It was my own fault. Mostly. Well, partly. I guess, looking back now, I can see how doctors handed out the drug like candy. How big Pharma was pushing the pills all in the name of money. But that only goes so far. As they tell us at group, we have to own our addiction."

"I hear that weekly."

"Same here." My finger slid up over his nose along the bridge. Now seemed the time to let him in fully. After all, he'd just admitted he was turning his entire life upside down. "I was in a group, small folk quintet, that had a sound. Something rare and pure. We'd been compared to the Mamas and the Papas. One music critic said I could be the next Sufjan Stevens, which is incredibly high praise." He smiled, and I knew he had no clue who Sufjan was. I would have to fix that. "Courtney—Leo's mom—was a fan I'd met in Fresno. We hit it right off. She moved in with me on the same day that a record company executive offered us a contract. We all signed on immediately. Folk acts don't get too many chances in today's music world. A tour was set up to back a new album. Opening night in Seattle, small club, maybe holding three hundred people. We'd been celebrating backstage. The west coast tour, the album, our good luck. The news that Courtney was carrying my child. Everything seemed to be right. The stars in alignment, the planets in harmony. Then, one misstep onstage ended it all. I fell. About ten feet. Twisting to try to right myself, I landed badly. Broke my arm and shattered a hip, tore my ACL so badly the surgeons took pictures as teaching aides."

"Shit, baby, I am sorry," Michael whispered, pulling me ever closer.

"Me too. I lost everything, except Courtney. My recovery would be lengthy, and the tour was already in the works. I told them to find a new singer. My bandmates did as asked, although they all wept while doing so. The record company gave me some money. I blew it all on pills. The nice house that my new wife and son lived in. Gone. My car. Gone. My career. Gone. All gone because of taking a long step, instead of a short one."

"You're an amazing soul, Bryce. I'm not a poet as you are—"

"Was."

"*Are*. But I know that you make me feel strong, happy, and able to face everything the world throws at me."

"You precious soul," I kissed his bare pectoral.

"Thank you for sharing that story with me. I know it hurt. The retellings. They always hurt."

"Mm, like reopening a mostly healed wound."

He nodded. We dozed. Then, his phone rang, pulling us out of that hazy place of dreams and memories. As soon as he took the call, his aura shifted from calm to tense. I lay beside him, listening to him grunt a few times, then tell whoever was on the other end he needed to think about it.

"Was that the team?" I chanced as he sat up to rub at his face with his hands.

"It was Jack. He and his partner, some guy named something weird…"

"Cormack. He's of Scottish descent. What do they want you to do?" A pang of unease flared up in my breast.

"Yeah, Cormack. They want me to come in for a chat, something about a meeting where I'm wired up."

"God above," I croaked, fear replacing unease in a heartbeat. "No, you can't do that. It's too dangerous. Tell them no. Let them find another way to nail Looper."

"I think I should do it," he whispered into the dark, his shoulders tight under the moonlight. "Jack said it will be safe. They'll be close. The wires are small now, the tech much better than in the old cop shows. I've seen it where they can put a mic in a button. That's crazy."

"So is thinking of going along with this."

"No, I think it's a good idea." He turned to face me and, even in the dark of night, with only the glow of the moon to illuminate the room, I could see that he was set. "It's the easiest way. They send me in, get him to confess to blackmail and doctoring the audio of what I said, and off he goes to prison. Then, he can't be harassing other people, extorting them, sending apes out to try to hurt old women and kids at the garden. I can't carry any more guilt. If Leo or the girls get hurt, I would not come back from it, Bryce."

As much as I hated it, I understood. I knew guilt personally. It clung to a soul like a leech.

"Are you sure?" I asked and got a nod. "When?"

"They'll let me know. I have to call them back."

"Okay."

"I love you."

"I love you. Now lie back down with me. I need you next to me for a little while longer."

Chapter 21

Michael

JACK EXPLAINED THE WORKINGS OF THE WIRE WITH CARE, all business. "You just need to get Looper talking. We need specific admissions—amounts, dates, anything concrete." I listened, the weight of the task settling on me. "Just act normal, and let him do the talking," Jack instructed. "We're counting on you to stay cool."

His gaze was intense, and I understood the importance of my role. Inside, I was a tangle of nerves. This wasn't just a conversation; it was a chess game, and I had to play my part to perfection.

"Are you sure this is what you want to do, Michael?" Jack asked me the same question he'd already asked twice, his tone serious.

I hesitated, the risks and what was at stake running through my mind. "Yeah, I'm sure. I've got to see this through," I replied, trying to sound more confident than I felt. The decision wasn't easy, but it was necessary. I knew this was a crucial step, not only for the case, but to close a chapter of my life. I wanted to start over; I wanted to keep addiction at bay; I wanted the garden; I wanted family; I wanted Bryce; and I wanted it all without shadows.

"Okay then," Jack nodded to his fellow officer, Cormack, who opened the door for me, and I stepped out of the car, two blocks from the same place I'd been the night when I'd lost the last of what I had.

The night Looper suggested I help throw a game and take the coward's way out for money.

Cormack touched my arm, a gesture of support, and then, it was done. They'd be listening and recording, but other than that, I was on my own.

I headed down the street, striding with purpose, shoulders back, and within a few minutes, I was at the unmarked door right next to the family restaurant. The scaffolding was gone, any evidence of me backing my car into the wall was gone, hell, no one would know what I'd done, but I could still picture that night—the win, the loss, the complete devastation caused by my temper, of how I'd hurt people.

For a second, I faltered and forced myself back to this morning, when Bryce, fresh from his shower, kissed me goodbye and made me promise to come back.

I'm coming back.

I'd promised him that, and it didn't matter how many goons were on the other side of this door, I would do what I needed to do and go home to the man I loved. Then, start all over with this new life I had. The door opened to reveal Kurgan, Looper's bodyguard, scowling out at me. He was just as big, tattooed, and intimidating as I remembered, and he eyed me with caution, scanning behind me before nodding and letting me in. His presence was a stark reminder of the world I was stepping back into, even if only for these few moments. The door shut behind us, and I blinked at the dim interior, walking past the room all set up with the round table where I'd lost the last of everything.

"Wait," Kurgan demanded, then did a cursory pat-down, something I'd been used to when I joined these underground high stakes games, taking out my cell phone and shoving it into a box. Then, he motioned for me to sit on a chair in a corridor—intimidation tactics 101—and I waited as long as they needed me to without checking my watch once. All too soon, he was back, gripping my arm and encouraging me down the hallway.

How had it come to this, that I was even in this situation?

Then, he gave me a not-so-gentle push into an office with a large desk and Looper sitting in a big chair like some kind of executive at a Wall Street firm, or a banker.

I stifled a hysterical laugh—a banker?—that was some funny shit.

"Come to give me my money, Zeetoo?"

"Michael," I corrected him. "And no, I don't have it."

He threw up a hand, and Kurgan crowded me. "Then, we have nothing to discuss. If you can't pay me, I'll get my kicks from releasing what I have on you."

I shook off Kurgan's hand but couldn't get away from him. Still, I guess being dragged from the room lent authenticity to what came next.

"I can get it, okay! You can't release a recording you've doctored so it will destroy me."

"I can, and I believe…" he consulted his damn notebook, ran a finger down the figures. "Let's call it a hundred thousand."

"I don't have that."

He leered at me, all white teeth and snarl. "I know. So, tell me what else you can do for me."

"Why?" I demanded, and this time, I managed to get my foot lodged against the table so I could shove Kurgan back, much to Looper's amusement.

"Why what?"

"You know I turned you down. You know I'd never let my team, my brother, down by causing a loss."

"Well of course I know that, but it's been fun, and who knows, you might go back to the Storm, and then, I'll have even more chances to take your money. And if you don't, then I'll leak it and get paid by the media, either way, I make, and you lose."

"It's not me on that recording."

He examined the notebook again. "But it is, Zeetoo.

234

It's you whimpering about just another twenty K, begging me, pleading, and then, refusing to throw a game like you're some kind of hero?"

There, I had that on the mic. "How did you do it? How did you make it sound as if I was willing to fuck everyone over?"

He sneered. "Anyone with connections can get all kinds of shit done."

"And those people in your book, that list of all those poor suckers that you've drawn in, and blackmailed—"

"Addicts like you are my bread and butter." He grinned, and I wanted to punch him in the mouth. "You all come here, 'just another ten, Looper', 'I'm good for it, Looper'. All so convinced you're going to win, borrowing money from me as if I can afford to let you leave with it? Then, all you do is lose, and boy, your losses feed my empire every single god-damned day."

"Fuck you!" I snapped.

He stood slowly, and I couldn't move as Kurgan dug his fingers into my neck.

"You're a fucking addict, Zeetoo, and you're nothing to me. And neither is your little garden friend and his kid, or your brother and his pretty blonde wife, not to mention those sweet little nieces of yours." I lurched forward, but Kurgan stopped me dead. "Your brother is fucking loaded, and if you don't get the money from him, I'll apply pressure and send in a crew. Then, you can fuck off and die for all I care."

"Don't you hurt my family."

"You don't get it, do you? I'll hurt who I want."

"I'll get the money," I blurted, and his eyes narrowed. "I want your assurance you won't hurt anyone, and you'll give me everything you recorded!" Blackness swum in my eyes when Kurgan's fingers dug deeper into my neck.

Jack never had a contingency plan for when this wannabe gangster decided to let his goon kill me.

You're nothing," Looper snapped. "And you're making my office untidy. Kurgan?"

I attempted to wriggle free, but Kurgan shoved me up against the doorjamb as he escorted me out, and all too soon, I was out in the sunlight, blinking and wheezing in pain. I waited until the door shut, then straightened, heading back the way I'd come, each step another one away from that life, the old Michael Zhang, the man desperate enough to have bargained for cash.

Would I've gotten to the point where I'd stolen to fund my addiction? Because it was for damned sure, I'd had no money left of my own.

My footsteps faltered, and I stopped outside a small grocery store, glanced in the window, and a bright poster for the lottery catching my eye. I could just…

Then, I recalled what I'd teased Charles with—telling him not to mention the lottery in group—and I smiled, then laughed, and then, I cried.

Right there on the street, in front of that store.

"It's okay: we've got you," a gruff voice explained,

and then, I felt an arm over my shoulder as Jack hustled me away. "You did good. We have enough for now. You're done."

"I'LL FIND HIM, AND THEN I'LL KILL HIM," BRYCE muttered as I removed my shirt, and he got first sight of the marks that Kurgan had left on me. My pacifist-vegetarian-zen-yoga-gardener was threatening death to a three hundred-pound bodyguard as he rubbed lotion around where the asshole had squeezed me. Jeez, it hurt.

"No, you won't," I murmured as he massaged the surrounding area, easing the bunched muscles until I could drop my shoulders. He'd been waiting here in his rooms over Mrs. Cho's for Jack to drop me off— something we'd arranged beforehand. I knew that I hadn't wanted to take any of this back to Charles and his family, and Bryce decided we'd meet here "so he could help me."

He'd understood the fear and the emotional toll I'd be working through, and just wanted to give me a safe space, and I loved him for that. He even had my sponsor on call, and Kevin had a quick chat with me, but I didn't want to think about addiction right now. I wanted to stop thinking about Looper and Kurgan, and the money, and the blackmail, and the scent of smoke and whiskey that'd become part of my compulsion.

"Jack says he can't arrest Looper yet," I added, "but

the recording goes along with other stuff to get a warrant for arrest and to search, and once he gets hold of the ledger and sees what happens in there—"

"Shhh," Bryce demanded. "I've got you."

I couldn't talk now anyway, Bryce kneading my flesh, kissing my neck, encouraging me to lean back in his arms, supporting me, with pillows behind us. I rested there a moment, a sense of complete peace in my head and my body, then I wriggled in his hold to face him, taking out one of the pillows so he was flatter and cuddling into his hold.

I was tired, and I think I told him that because he chuckled and shifted only a little to bring the blanket up over the two of us.

"You're so brave," he murmured.

"It's not brave to lose everything and blame anyone but myself for how I got there. It's not brave to destroy family."

He pressed a kiss to my temple. "Maybe not, but it's brave to admit you're an addict, and work your way back to being the man you really are. That's brave." His words struck a note. I'd never felt like battling my addiction was a brave thing, more a necessity, given the one-track road I'd been following. I'd lost everything, and how much longer could I have gone on?

"I think you're brave too. You're my hero," I whispered against his chest, burrowing deeper, his arms wrapped around me.

"I'm no hero," he laughed, and I could hear his heart under my ear, and the gruffness of his chuckle.

"You've taken me on, right?" I asked.

"I guess having to deal with you makes me kind of heroic," he teased.

I lifted my head to stare into his eyes. "Yep. My hero."

Epilogue

Bryce

"Come on, ref, what, are you blind?!"

"Dad, chill out, it was a legit hit. Clean shoulder check."

I glanced down at Leo, suited up for his turn on the ice with the youth league following this early-as-all-sin veteran game. He was a forward, rather good if I did say so myself. He had a few good teachers after all.

"Right, sure, sorry." I sat down just as Michael—all kinds of sexy and coach-like behind the bench for the San Pedro Predators vet team—glanced over his shoulder at me. He smiled and shook his head. I shrugged, then sat next to my son. "Who knew hockey could be this stirring?" I saw the *doh* in my son's eyes. Of course. Everyone knew hockey and karate were the bee's knees. How silly of me. "Did you bring your mouthguard?"

"Yes," he sighed, then wiggled over a few seats to

chat with the other kids on his team. All in purple as they were the Storm's sponsored group.

"Good man," I said to myself. According to Michael it was important that young hockey players learn to bring all their own equipment as well as carry it into the rink. I had to mentally—and physically at times—slap my hand to quit reaching for his gear bag to check if it was packed properly with all his necessities. If it wasn't, he would sit out a game. The coach was fair, but firm about that, and Michael agreed.

Leaning back to sip some cocoa with mini marshmallows, I found my sight drifting from the ice to my boyfriend. We'd been a couple now for over a year. I had never been happier. Especially now that all that nasty stuff with Looper was in the past.

"Hey," I heard Jack say as he dropped down into a hard plastic seat, his cheeks covered with thick whiskers, his hair a mess, with dark bags under his eyes. "Seriously, why the hell do they schedule games at this time? What kind of purgatory is this?"

"This is a busy rink. They have over fifteen leagues of varying—"

"Yep, you can stop chattering at me now. I've only had a few sips of this coffee, and I'm out of smokes." He held up a Minnie Mouse thermos with a cracked pink plastic cup.

"You should quit," I said and got the same eye roll I always got from him. We'd grown a bit closer since he had come through for Michael in such a big way.

"I will, just as soon as all the cases on my desk are closed."

Which meant never. Seemed there was always a lesser slime ball waiting to ascend the ladder of organized crime. When Looper and his men had been incarcerated, fifteen more criminals were vying for Looper's little throne, according to Jack. And he would know.

"They make gum that you can chew that's supposed—"

"Shhhhh now, I'm watching the men make hockey." He twisted off the cracked cup, poured some black coffee into it, drank it down, and promptly fell asleep. With an eye roll, I plucked the cup from his fingers, took care of the thermos, and tossed the blanket from my lap over his chest.

Now that Jack was napping, and Leo was with his team giggling over something his teammate Carmen had said about a cartoon, I could devote myself to the game. And the handsome coach who would be coming home with me in three hours. Ugh, my toes were cold already. They'd be little frozen piggies come noon. Such was the life of a gardening dad who was in love with a volunteer coach. I wouldn't change a thing. Well, other than having the ice rink be warmer. That would make this a community pool, and not an ice rink.

Michael was deep in conversation with one of the linesmen about a call he hadn't liked. Not the check. That was clean. My son knew stuff. But an icing call

I'd missed while tucking in Jack. Courtney would be so proud of the progress her brother and I had made. She and Tony were on their honeymoon. Three weeks touring state parks after a lovely little ceremony in Yellowstone. They'd left yesterday, after spending a day and night in a rustic cabin in the woods. Michael and I were thrilled to have Leo for the time away. He could do his schoolwork online while I was tending to the garden and those who visited it daily.

Michael still lived in the pool house, but he was searching for his own place to rent, doing some training sessions for cash with a local gym. He'd progressed enough in his therapy that he felt ready to take on more independence. More, in this case, meaning a home close to the garden so my commute wouldn't be too lengthy. So, not just his place, but *our* place. We were going to move in together as soon as the perfect home could be located. I'd miss my little place above Mrs. Cho, but it was time for me to take a few long overdue first steps. Perhaps not first steps, but more like getting back to where I'd been when I'd stumbled so badly off life's path. With Michael by my side. the woods seemed less foreboding and the direction more certain.

I dug into my pocket for my phone, then hurried to type out a few lines for a song I'd been working on. I had a folder full of them. Brand new. With music to go with the lyrics. I'd even reached out to my old agent,

Bradley, who had been so thrilled to hear I was well, clean, and possibly thinking about recording again.

I glanced up to see Michael waving his arms, still chatting to the linesman who by his body language was close to tossing Michael from the game. My man had a mad passion for hockey whether it be when he watched the Storm or like now, behind the bench with this vets' team. He might not have gone back to the Storm, but there was no way he would ever leave the game forever. And that was fine. We all had to navigate our way through the forest on our own unique paths.

Hmm, perhaps that new album could be titled Finding my way through the woodland or something like that. I'd run that past Bradley to see what he thought about it. I felt the weight of Michael staring at me. My gaze lifted from my phone, and yep, there were those loving eyes resting on me. He fake-strummed a guitar. His silent way of asking if I was working on music. I nodded. He grinned.

The man was my biggest fan, even bigger than my ex-wife and her new husband. Leo thought my songs were kind of lame, but he was nearly nine and wasn't going to be impressed with my creative endeavors unless they had to do with sports, video games, or echidnas. He was hell bent on owning an echidna. Why? No clue. Michael questioned me about the anteater desire daily, and I told him to wait it out. In six months, it would be a different pet. Maybe, when we found our new home, we could discuss getting a pet. Not an echidna though. I wasn't sure you could even own one in LA County.

A cat would be nice. A rescue needing some love and a nice home. Maybe that tuxedo tom cat that hung round the garden would like to come inside and get affection. I'd discuss it with him the next time he was prowling through the corn stalks. The cat, not Michael. Him, I would talk to when we had a home to bring a cat into.

When I glanced up next, Leo and his gang were shuffling to the ice, and the adult game was ending. Michael exited the bench wearing a smile. I peeked at the score, shamefaced that I'd missed out on the final ten minutes with my head in the musical clouds.

I elbowed Jack. He started awake, blinked, and threw me a dark glare.

"The boys will be on the ice next," I told him. The aggravation at being woken left his face. The man adored his nephew. Which, I felt, was part of the reason he'd gone after Looper as aggressively as he had. Not that he didn't go after all felons with vigor, but if someone endangered Leo, they'd have one irate cop on their ass.

"Cool. I need more coffee." He plucked the Minnie thermos from the cement floor, rose with a groan, and ambled off, using the blanket as a cape. You would think the man would know to dress warmer when coming to the ice rink. He was here every Saturday that Leo played, or Michael coached.

Returning to my song, I shot into the air gasping when someone kissed the back of my neck, then smiling as I felt familiar lips skimming along to my ear. "You start nibbling, and this family time will quickly turn into something less G-rated."

He gave the earrings in my lobe a quick tug, then crawled over the seat to my left and sat down with a sigh. His tie was gone, probably in his jacket pocket, and his dress shirt was unbuttoned to show just enough pale skin and freckles to be tempting.

"Well done on the win."

"Thanks. I think we're coming along. We might actually make the playoffs this season." I nodded and offered him my hot chocolate thermos. He shook his head. He was not a fan of marshmallows. Said he hated the squeak they made on his teeth when he chewed them. I had informed him that you swallowed, something he was exceptionally good at, but he was having none of that. I loved the man and all his little quirks, even the marshmallow one. "Did you get that song done?"

"Mm, mostly. I need an ending. A happy one. I want this album to reflect where I am in my life right now."

His gaze moved from the kids hitting the ice to me, a warm glow in those depths that always made me feel tingly inside.

"I make you happy?"

"Incredibly so."

He stole a kiss. "I'm happy too. Did you check your

emails? Sharon sent us a slimmed-down list of available properties to look at. You want to do that after we're done here? Maybe grab some lunch with Leo, then check out houses?"

"Sure, but we have to stop at the garden first to help with the fall harvest. Oh, and then we have that meeting with Hal and Clare at four about the affordable housing initiative. They might have narrowed the land choices for mini-homes down to two lots that might come close to the funds we've raised."

"I hope we can lure a few local carpenters in to donate some man-hours," he sat back, then waved at Leo as he skated a lap with his team. "He's much sharper on his corners now. I knew working with him during the week would help."

I wiggled my fingers at my son as he raced by, cheeks pink, eyes bright. "He thinks you walk on water; you know that?"

"He's a kid. I mean… he wants an anteater for a pet."

"Mm, well, anteaters on leashes aside, the boy has a good eye for good people."

He chuckled. "You're going to make me say it, aren't you? Right here in front of everyone and your brother-in-law. Hey Jackson."

He'd gotten out of repeating one of the many affirmations he recited daily. He *was* a damned good man.

"Hey Mikey Z." Jack sat down on my right,

stretched out his legs, and hooted at Leo taking a quick shot at the empty net. The puck soared high and wide, cracking into the glass. "Maybe you need to work on accuracy with the boy."

Michael rolled his eyes, looped an arm around my shoulder, and pecked me on the cheek.

"I love you despite that ballbuster on your right," he fake-whispered loud enough for Jack to hear. Jackson huffed into his drink.

"As long as you love me, we can handle the ballbuster," I replied, cuddling close into his side.

We'd walked through the darkest wood. But we'd come out into a sun drenched clearing, hand in hand, to feel the warmth of love on our faces.

With his love in my heart, we could handle whatever the world threw at us.

What's next for the LA Storm?

Shield (LA Storm, 3)

Can Jackson ensure the safety of his loved ones when the darkest elements of LA's underbelly seek retribution?

Oliver knows the clock is ticking on his dream of winning the Stanley Cup. After fourteen years playing for New York, he's beyond frustrated to leave friends behind when traded to the LA Storm. As a widower and father of two girls, he's facing the twilight of his career, and, worst of all, he's lonely. Making friends is easy enough, but he craves someone to hold him at night. When Jackson, equal parts grumpy chaos and charm, lands in his life, friendship turns to lust, and love isn't far behind. He finds himself drawn to Jackson, and as their relationship deepens, they become each other's haven amidst the chaos of their lives. However, danger from Jackson's work threatens their peaceful world, challenging their relationship and forcing love to take a backseat to survival.

After bringing down a notable money launderer, Jackson's small team receives orders to delve deeper into the world of organized crime in Hollywood. His early success quickly spirals into an overwhelming web of criminal intrigue. In this new, uncharted territory, he feels increasingly isolated, both personally and professionally. The more issues he uncovers, the less he seems to close. Meeting Oliver shakes his world even more, especially when he accidentally falls for the widower and father of two little girls. A few nights of fun is one thing, but deeper feelings and kids are something he is not at all prepared for. Yet, despite his reluctance, he becomes deeply attached to the little family who has embraced him with so much love. Now, he just has to shield them from the dangers that have followed him to their doorstep.

This opposites attract romance features a single dad hockey player grappling with personal loss, a grumpy detective entangled in the complexities of organized crime, and a love story that happens despite the odds.

Hockey Series' from RJ Scott & V.L. Locey

Harrisburg Railers

Owatonna U Hockey

Arizona Raptors

Boston Rebels

LA Storm

Chesterford Coyotes - Young Adult

Harrisburg Railers

When hockey wunderkind Tennant Rowe meets his new coach, he knows he's in trouble. Jared Madsen is nine years older than Tennant, impossibly attractive, and — worst of all — his brother's off-limits best friend. Is their chemistry worth the risk?

Changing Lines (Railers 1)

Can Tennant show Jared that age is just a number, and that love is all that matters?

The Rowe Brothers are famous hockey hotshots, but as the youngest of the trio, Tennant has always had to play against his brothers' reputations. To get out of their shadows, and against their advice, he accepts a trade to the Harrisburg Railers, where he runs into Jared Madsen. Mads is an old family friend and his brother's one-time teammate. Mads is Tennant's new coach. And Mads is the sexiest thing he's ever laid eyes on.

Jared Madsen's hockey career was cut short by a fault in his heart, but coaching keeps him close to the game. When Ten is traded to the team, his carefully organized world is thrown into chaos. Nine years his junior and his best friend's brother, he knows Ten is strictly off-limits, but as soon as he sees Ten's moves, on and off the ice, he knows that his heart could get him into trouble again.

———

Harrisburg Railers (Hockey Romance)

1. Changing Lines
2. First Season
3. Deep Edge
4. Poke Check
5. Last Defense
6. Goal Line
7. Neutral Zone
8. Hat Trick
9. Save The Date
10. Baby Makes Three
11. Rivals
12. Perfect Gifts
13. Family First

Railers Volume 1 | Railers Volume 2 | Railers Volume 3 | Railers Volume 4

Owatonna U, College Hockey

Meet the men of Owatonna University's hockey team

Ryker (Owatonna U, 1)

Ryker is hockey royalty, Jacob is a poor country boy. Can two vastly different people find common ground and become the men they want to be?

Ryker comes from a long line of championship-winning hockey players. Playing college hockey to develop his game is his only focus, and nothing will stand in the way of him working to become the best player. He has no room for relationships, people who point out his flaws, or anyone who calls him on his dreams. He certainly has no place for love, and meeting Jacob is nothing but a useful distraction on the side. After all trying to get his Owatonna Eagles teammate into bed is less work and more play. When tragedy rocks his family, his charmed life crumbles, and the only person he can turn to is the same one who claims to hate him.

Jacob Benson has only known hard work and stifling conservative values his whole life. Born and raised in the small rural community of Eden Crossing, Minnesota, he's the only son of a hard-working but struggling dairy farming family. Jacob is using his skills in hockey to finance his way to an agricultural science degree. These four years at Owatonna U. will probably be the only time he has to enjoy life, gain acceptance about his sexuality, and live openly before his inevitable return to the farm. Running into a pretty rich boy like Ryker Madsen is putting a damper on his enjoyment of life away from home. Ryker's flip, conceited, carefree attitude grates on Jacob's every nerve. So why, if Ryker is everything he dislikes, does he want nothing more than to explore the sinful dreams that his annoying teammate stars in every night?

Ryker

Owatonna U Hockey (Hockey Romance)

1. Ryker

Arizona Raptors

Coast to Coast (Arizona Raptors 1)

Coast To Coast

When opposites attract, this bottom-of-the-league team will never be the same again.

A stipulation in his father's will forces Mark back into the arms of a family that disowned him and leaves him one-third owner of a hockey team facing financial ruin. He doesn't even watch hockey, let alone like it, and wants nothing more than to head back to New York. Then there's the new coach, a stubborn, opinionated, irritating man with superiority issues and questionable music taste. Butting heads with Rowen becomes the new normal, but it comes with passionate debate and an all-consuming lust.

Challenged to rebuild one of the worst teams in the league into a future cup contender, Rowen can't pass up the opportunity. Never in his twenty years of hockey has he ever seen a team managed so badly or coached players overflowing with resentment and bigotry. Yet there's something about this team and this city that compels him to roll up his sleeves and start dismantling. If only Mark, one of three siblings who now own the Raptors, wasn't so damned rock-headed yet so damned appealing his job might be easier. It doesn't look like either is willing to give in, but one night in a dark, desert hotel changes everything.

Coast To Coast

Arizona Raptors (Hockey Romance)

1. Coast To Coast
2. Across the Pond
3. Shadow and Light
4. Sugar and Ice
5. School and Rock

Boston Rebels

Top Shelf (Boston Rebels 1)

Acting on the attraction to his best friend's brother has always been off the table for Xander until a passionate hookup with Mason at a beach resort begins a love affair that burns long after summer ends.

Mason specializes in assisting same-sex couples on their journey to becoming parents and fighting every rule that blocks his way in the stuck-in-the-past agency that hired him. Living in his brother's pool house is rent-free, and every cent he earns he saves for his dream—that one day he'd have his own company helping others. The downside is that he has to see his annoying brother every day, the upside is that his brother's teammates from the Boston Rebels make regular visits. The eye candy that passes Mason's window is almost enough to make him consider dating a hockey player, but not just any player though. Ever since Xander—his brother's childhood friend—came out as gay at a press conference, Mason's puppy love has turned into a burning attraction he can no longer ignore.

Hockey has been one of Xander's main focuses since he was old enough to balance on skates. Well, hockey and Mason Kingsley, but Mason was always unattainable. Now that he's about to see thirty candles on his birthday cake and is no longer hiding the fact he's gay, he's ready to find a soul mate to make his life complete. A summer vacation is just what he needs to have time to think, but when the Boston Rebels arriving in paradise with Mason in tow, thinking is the last thing he needs. One torrid night under a balmy moon and rules about not messing with his best friend's brother vanish on a warm, tropical breeze.

Summer romances don't generally last past Labor Day, but with the new season about to begin Xander and Mason are going to have to face the world and decide if their love is real enough to withstand everything.

Boston Rebels

Lost In Boston (Free Prequel Novella)

1. Top Shelf

Chesterford Coyotes, Young Adult Romance

Off The Ice (Chesterford Coyotes, 1)

Off The Ice

A coming-of-age love story with high school, hockey rivalry, friendship, family, and coming out.

Soren's life changes in an instant when he and his younger brother are adopted by hockey royalty. Making sense of his new life is hard enough, but when he's enrolled in a private school it means facing a whole new set of problems. Navigating friendship, family, and hockey is one thing, but being attracted to the boy who vexes him is a whole new thing.

Felix has a reputation to protect. He's the kid who seems to have everything but looks can be deceiving. Spinning lies about his perfect life, he's created a fantasy world that even he has started to believe. Only, it's not long before everything crumbles, all of his pretty lies are revealed, and only his closest rival sees through his pain and stands by him.

Fighting is easy, friendship is hard, but love is everything.

Off The Ice

Chesterford Coyotes

Also By RJ Scott

For a full list of ebooks and links please scan the code above
or visit rjscott.co.uk/rjbooks

Meet RJ Scott

RJ discovered romance in books at a very young age and realized that if there wasn't romance on the page, she could create it in her head. With over one hundred and fifty books published, she is a full time author of gay romance.

She lives and works out of her home in the beautiful English countryside, spends her spare time reading, watching films, and enjoying time with her family.

The last time she had a week's break from writing she didn't like it one little bit and has yet to meet a box of chocolates she couldn't defeat.

www.rjscott.co.uk | rj@rjscott.co.uk

NEWSLETTER - rjscott.co.uk/rjnews

facebook.com/author.rjscott

x.com/Rjscott_author

instagram.com/rjscott_author

amazon.com/author/rj-scott

bookbub.com/authors/rj-scott

goodreads.com/rjscott

pinterest.com/rjscottauthor

Also By VL Locey

For a full list of ebooks and links please scan the code above
or visit vllocey.com/stories-from-vl-locey

Meet V.L. Locey

V.L. Locey loves worn jeans, yoga, belly laughs, walking, reading and writing lusty tales, Greek mythology, the New York Rangers, comic books, and coffee.

(Not necessarily in that order.)

She shares her life with her husband, her daughter, one dog, two cats, a flock of assorted domestic fowl, and two Jersey steers.

When not writing spicy romances, she enjoys spending her day with her menagerie in the rolling hills of Pennsylvania with a cup of fresh java in hand.

vllocey.com
vicki@vllocey.com

Newsletter - vllocey.com/newsletter

facebook.com/V.L.Locey

x.com/vllocey

instagram.com/vl_locey

bookbub.com/authors/v-l-locey

goodreads.com/vllocey

pinterest.com/vllocey